"SHE DID *WHAT* TO THE CAR?"
HER FATHER YELLED.

Clutching her necklace, she closed her eyes and braced herself. . . .

"Oh, please," she heard herself murmur. "Please, please take me away."

Then she began to feel peculiar, slightly dizzy, almost queasy. . . . She reached out to steady herself, and a strange, loud *whoosh* seemed to envelop her.

She opened her eyes, but the room was dark.

As her eyes adjusted to the dimness, she heard the crackling of a fire.

Then someone coughed.

Immediately she whirled around. Across a vast room she saw a boy about her own age, wrapped in what appeared to be a very thick bathrobe with fur on the collar. . . .

Then he looked at her, raising his pale eyebrows. "I have been awaiting your visit."

Sam was about to ask him who he was, how she got there, when she recognized him.

He was Edward VI, the boy king of England. And he had been dead for almost five hundred years.

SIMON PULSE
New York London Toronto Sydney Singapore

First Simon Pulse edition February 2002

SIMON PULSE
An imprint of Simon & Schuster
Children's Publishing Division
1230 Avenue of the Americas
New York, NY 10020

The text of this book was set in Goudy Old Style.
Book design by Sammy Yuen Jr.
Printed in United States of America
10 9 8 7 6 5 4 3 2 1

Library of Congress Control Number: 2001096492

ISBN 0-7434-1921-9

This book is for all of the kids I'm lucky enough to have in my life, mostly through my son Seth. And mostly through the kitchen. . . . Tom, Zachary, Philip, Semut, Jonah, Ned, John, and David. And for the girls, Aislinn, Nora, and Gilly.

Finally, for Nicole, a real-life fairy princess who can toss a water balloon with the best of 'em.

Prologue

Many hundreds of years ago, in a distant time and land, there lived a very powerful magician. Although he used his art to perform good deeds, there came a day when he realized his magic had become stronger than he was. No longer could he control his own powers. For the great magician had discovered the secrets to time itself.

Frightened by the unbridled sorcery and what it could do to the world, he moved to a smaller village far from his home and relinquished his claim to all things mystical. There, through hard work and mighty resolution, he became a silversmith of great renown. Kings and queens craved his wares, for they were exquisitely wrought, and the silver in them glistened like diamonds.

After a short time, though, the magician discovered that his silver works were endowed with the same mystical gifts he had attempted to quell. Swiftly he gathered up all of his works, promising the owners that he would make their treasures even more magnificent.

Instead, he destroyed his own mastepieces. Content at last, he lived out his remaining years in peace.

He had forgotten one solitary silver plate, and decades later, during a time of violence and chaos in his land, that plate was melted down in a large vat of silver. The mystical essence of the magician's powers was turned into hundreds of other bits of silver, from candlesticks to cups, from small charms to spoons.

For the most part the silver is safe, the strength of the sorcery diluted and diffused. On rare occasions, however, the magic in the piece takes over. When a special person holds the precious metal and wishes hard enough—even without knowing what can occur—the power that the wise magician so dreadfully feared returns.

That is precisely what has happened. . . .

Chapter 1

Samantha McKenna knew the moment she looked at her best friend's face that something had gone wrong. Terribly wrong.

"Lori," Samantha began, reaching up to touch her own hair. It felt like straw. "Please, give me the mirror."

Lori's eyes remained wide and fixed as she hid the hand mirror behind her back. "But it said to leave the highlighter on for forty-five minutes, didn't it?"

Panic began to rise in Samantha's throat. "I don't know. You told me that's how long you left it on, and your hair looks great. The mirror, Lori. I need to know."

"Maybe we shouldn't have done it right after the perm. Maybe that's the problem. It just seemed logical, to perm and highlight together. A real step saver. Didn't it seem logical to you?"

The front door slammed downstairs.

"Anyone home?" It was Jason, Sam's ten-year-old brother.

"We're upstairs in my room," Sam shouted. "Please, Lori." The unmistakable clumping thud of Jason's roller blades on the steps seemed to rattle the entire house. Then came the sliding hum of the skates on the carpet after he reached the landing.

"Hey, Sam, is there anything to eat. I'm . . ." Jason stopped midsentence as he glided past her door. Then he pulled up short, gripped the doorknob, and pulled himself back.

"Don't you dare say anything," Lori warned.

He didn't have to. The expression on his face said it all. It was the same expression as Lori's, one of shocked disbelief. The dirty bandage cupped on his chin, dangling on one end, exaggerated his open mouth.

"What happened?" He did not laugh, did not make a joke. That's when Samantha realized it was even worse than she had feared.

"We gave her a home perm and a few highlights." Lori was unable to pull her gaze from Sam's frizzled head. "We were going for that rumpled look that's in all the magazines. You know, casual curls. Like that girl in the TV show about troubled teens."

Jason's traitorous eyes crinkled, and then he

grinned, exposing the multicolored rubber bands on the braces on his teeth. "Troubled teens? Sam, with hair like yours . . ."

"That's enough." Samantha mustered all the dignity she could and walked to her dresser mirror. "Oh," she whispered.

"I'll bet if we put on a ton of conditioner, it'll be fine," Lori offered in a tone that indicated she didn't believe a word of it.

Samantha simply stared at the bleached nightmare in the reflection. Less than two hours earlier she had been a sleek-haired brunette, eagerly anticipating her sixteenth birthday party in a couple of days, dreaming of getting her driver's license. Now all she could see was a mass of frizzy hair streaked with shocks of white. "Oh," she repeated.

"Hey, clown head," Jason chuckled. "I'd stay away from matches if I were you. Your head'll go up like a torch."

"Don't you have someplace else to go?" Lori snapped.

"Nah. Hey, Sam, is there anything for me to eat around here?"

Sam was still incapable of coherent speech, so Lori replied.

"We've got some doughnuts downstairs. Why don't you go and stuff your mouth with them? Then you won't be able to talk."

"I can't, brainiac. I'm allergic to wheat. Come on, Sam. I'm starving here."

"I'll have to cancel my party." Sam touched the remains of what had been her hair. "There's no way anyone can see me like this, especially not . . ." She stopped and shot her brother a warning look.

"What. You mean Kevin the Hunk?" Jason teased. He had fully recovered from the horror of Sam's hair.

"It's not so bad, really." Lori stood behind her friend, unable to keep the grimace from her face. "Hey, I have an idea."

"Snacks?" Jason offered helpfully.

"No. Remember that ad in last month's *Seventeen*?"

"For snacks?" Jason asked.

Ignoring him, Lori continued. "It was for some new product, a deep conditioner. Said it repaired dried and damaged hair. I saw it at Farley's Drug the other day."

"Really?" Sam said, just a flicker of hope beginning to emerge.

"They have snacks there, too," Jason added.

"Yeah!" Lori's enthusiasm was rising. "Okay," she checked her watch. "It's ten till five. They close at five, but we can still make it if we get a move on."

Sam smiled. "Great! I'll get a scarf for my head and . . ." The smile faded.

"What's wrong?" Lori had already grabbed her purse.

"How will we get there? It's more than a mile away."

All three paused, then Lori brightened. "Your dad's car!"

"No way!" Sam exclaimed. Her father's new metallic blue BMW was in the garage, tucked under a protective cloth. It had been a family joke that her dad had been sleeping in the garage to be closer to his car. When he left on a business trip two days earlier, her mom had presented him with wallet-size photos of the car, and he had immediately slipped them into his wallet. Sam knew the one thing she could not possibly do was drive the new car. "I only have my learner's permit anyway."

"But this is an emergency," Lori reasoned. "It will only take a few seconds. I'll even run into the store—you don't even have to park, which I know is an issue with you."

"Only parallel parking."

"Right. Come on, Sam. Do you want to go another day like this? Maybe the conditioner will work better the sooner we get it on your head. We've got to hurry!"

She shouldn't, she knew she really shouldn't. One more glance at her disastrous hair and she realized it was, indeed, an emergency. Her mom wasn't due back from work for another hour. No one would know. Except . . .

"Jason, you have to swear you won't tell anyone."

"No problem. As long as you let me have a few snacks."

There was no time to negotiate. "Fine. Let's go."

They tore down the steps, Jason clunking, insisting that he come along. A sense of high adventure gripped them all.

Sam was oh-so careful, just like the cautious drivers in the driver's ed videos. She adjusted the rearview mirror, moved the seat up, and with great deliberation turned the key to the ignition.

The motor started, a great, powerful rumbling sound that delighted her father and made Sam want to cringe.

"Seat belts, everyone?"

"Seat belts?" Jason said from the backseat. "You kidding? I have a parachute and a crash helmet back here."

She backed out of the garage and driveway slowly, biting her lip. Lori leaned over and hunted for the radio buttons.

"No radio!" Sam all but shouted.

"I was just . . ."

"No radio!"

"She needs to hear the police sirens when they pull her over," Jason said, grinning.

Sam didn't bother to answer. By the second block, it wasn't so bad. There was barely any traffic on the suburban streets, and the wooden steering wheel seemed comforting and secure. Her death grip on the wheel relaxed a little. She stopped smoothly and completely at each stop sign, looked both ways, and even smiled at another driver.

In a few moments they were at the drugstore. As if the trip was destined to be, the entire curb in front of the store was clear of cars and people. Even the expanse fronting the supermarket next door was empty. It was all wide open, a welcoming bastion of space to beckon beginning drivers.

"Just pull up here," Lori instructed. "I'll run in."

"Me, too," Jason began to push the front seat forward. "Snacks."

Lori started to protest, but Sam waved

her on. "Let him go. I'll be right here."

Sam eased the car into PARK and began her wait. They should be back home in less than ten minutes. The hum of the engine made her smile, and she leaned her left arm casually on the door.

What was taking them so long?

Then she glanced at the radio. A few tunes would be great right about now. She flicked the ON button, and her dad's oldies station came on. Smiling, she leaned forward to switch to her station, then fiddled with the fine tuning buttons. She couldn't get it right, though, there was static just as her favorite song began to play.

Then she glanced up at the rearview mirror. Another car had pulled up right behind her. "Darn," she mumbled. Couldn't he have gone someplace else? With all the space, he really didn't need to get so close.

She was thinking of inching forward when she saw Lori and Jason emerge from the store. Lori held up a brown paper bag in triumph, Jason was busy chewing something. Just then a young woman with a stroller walked right in front of the car, a harried, distracted expression on her face. The toddler in the stroller tossed something on the pavement, and the mother stopped to pick it up, resting a hand on the hood of the BMW.

Sam made a mental note to remove her handprints from the hood when they got home.

Still smiling, she looked over at Lori and Jason, but they had stopped walking. A strange look was on their faces, and Jason was no longer chewing. Instead his mouth was half open. Sam was about to ask them what was wrong when it became all too apparent.

A fully loaded shopping cart was careening straight for the passenger side of her car.

Behind the cart was a blur of someone in a red apron yelling and running, but unable to catch the runaway cart. Groceries tumbled as it picked up speed going down the ramp from the supermarket toward the drugstore curb.

It all happened in a split second. The young mother with the stroller was still in front of her, the other car right behind. There was no place for Sam to move. She was trapped.

There was absolutely nothing for her to do but close her eyes and wince.

Sam swallowed hard as she replaced the drop cloth on the BMW.

"When does your dad get back from his

trip?" Lori asked, clutching the now-forgotten bag with two boxes of conditioner.

"Tonight."

"Oh."

Jason skated a small circle in the garage, a handful of popcorn in his mouth. "Well, Sam, it's been nice having you as a sister."

"Be quiet," Sam snapped. Then she stared at Lori. "How could this have happened?"

"A runaway shopping cart crashed into the side of the car," Jason explained. "Funny. The cart wasn't even dented. I never knew a little shopping cart could mess up a new BMW so easily."

"Maybe your dad won't look at the car for a couple of days."

"That will be the first thing he does," Sam moaned. "Before he kisses my mom or asks how my math test was, he'll check on the car."

"Well," Lori handed Sam the conditioner. "I've got to get home now."

"Hey, Lori"—Jason grinned—"need a ride?"

Then they heard the sound of Sam's mother's car pulling into the driveway, and even Jason looked nervous.

"I've gotta go," Lori began to leave, then stopped. "It will be fine, really. Remember what Mr. Novack said in history class? 'No ten-year significance.' That's how you know if something you did is important, if it still makes a difference in ten years. And this little dent or two has absolutely no ten-year significance, right?"

"Right," Sam said quietly. But it wasn't a dent. The whole side of the car looked as if it had collapsed. Lori smiled with a quiver and left through the side door of the garage.

For a few moments Jason and Sam simply stared at each other.

"Anyone home?" Their mother called from the kitchen.

Before Sam could answer, Jason called, "We're in the garage, Mom. Guess what Sam did!"

It was the beginning of a very long night.

Her mother had been great.

After the initial shock of seeing Sam's hair, followed by the second shock of seeing the BMW resembling a folded accordion, her mom said at least no one had been hurt. That was the important thing.

But the way she kept repeating it made Sam suspect her mother was trying to convince herself. She checked her watch every few minutes, as if preparing herself for the moment Sam's dad found out what had happened to his car.

Sam sat on her bed, her hair still damp from the conditioner. It had helped a little, especially the second application. Instead of frizzy white hair, she had intensely curly, somewhat lightened hair. Her mother said it brought out her eyes. Jason said that was a good thing—with her eyes out, she wouldn't have to see their dad go ballistic.

She was flopped on her stomach, elbows propped up, her chin supported in her hands, a thick history book open to the middle Tudors. All of the words ran together as she tried to concentrate, to think about her test the next day. The last thing she needed was to compound the dented BMW with a failing history grade.

"Middle Tudors," she said aloud. The pictures were lovely, full color and lush, of stiff-faced people in uncomfortable-looking velvet clothes. Some of the women wore hoods, some triangular like little houses, others rounded. At least they covered their hair, lucky things.

Her focus kept returning to the crumpled car in the garage, not to the Tudors.

There was a gentle knock on her door, and her mother entered.

"How are you doing?"

"Fine. Just studying for my history test." She stared intently at the book, hoping her mother would go away and leave her alone.

Her mom nodded. "Your hair looks much better, Sam."

"Yeah, thanks. My hair looks better, but the car's a mess."

"Honey, you know it was wrong to have taken Dad's car. You don't have your license yet. You could have been hurt, or hurt someone else."

"I know."

"Well . . ."

Sam tugged on the sleeve of her white cotton nightgown, her neck still bent toward the book. Why was her mom just hanging out in the doorway?

Finally her mother cleared her throat. "This is a little early, but I thought you could use some cheering up." She handed her an oblong box.

Sam sat up. "What is it?"

"An almost-sixteen birthday present. Go ahead, open it."

Sam hesitated for a moment, then opened the box. Inside was a beautiful silver chain with a single strange-looking charm. It was round, with ornate piercings and a hollow center, as if it should be filled with something. It looked a little like a small Christmas ornament, or one of those painted eggs people put on display shelves.

"Oh, Mom," Sam said. "I love it!"

"Here, let me help you." Her mother lifted her hair and fastened the clasp around her neck. "I found it at an antique shop in town. I don't know why, but it reminded me of you. I've had it for months."

"It's wonderful." Sam sighed, looking down at the silver necklace against her nightgown. "Mom, thank you," she reached up and hugged her mother.

"You're welcome, Sam, and don't worry. Everything will be fine with your dad."

Then her mother left the room, and Sam returned to her studying, fingering the necklace as she read. It was beautiful, the necklace. It even felt beautiful, strangely warm and smooth.

The Middle Tudors.

After the great King Henry VIII died in 1547, his young son Edward became king. King Henry, the big bearded guy with all the wives, was actually a dad. What would he do to punish his kid?

Lucky Edward, she thought. He didn't have

to worry about fender benders or frizzy hair or history tests. The portrait of the young King Edward showed a sort of cute guy in a way-too fancy outfit. There were jewels and feathers and furs all over his hat and doublet, and his fingers were stacked with rings like those of a hostess on the Home Shopping Network.

Was that lace collar his idea? she wondered.

She began to read about him, this lucky Edward. Actually, she sort of got into his story, the tale of a young English king hundreds of years ago. He was almost exactly her age when he died.

What had it been like to live back then? To be a king at fifteen?

And then she heard the front door open.

Her father was home.

Although she couldn't hear the words, she could hear the sounds of the conversation. Her mother's voice, calm, friendly. Then Jason went down the steps.

"Hey, Dad. Guess what Sam did!"

Sam held her breath, staring at the painting of Edward, wishing she could just take the entire afternoon away and start over. Lucky Edward. No wonder he looked so calm in the picture. The guy didn't have a problem in the world.

"She did WHAT to the car?" her father yelled.

Clutching her necklace, she closed her eyes and braced herself for her father's wrath.

How she longed to be someplace else, anyplace else!

"Oh, please," she heard herself murmur. "Please, please take me away."

With all of her might, caught in a frenzy of irrational longing, she focused her entire being on that one simple thought. To be away. To be gone, right now.

Then she began to feel peculiar, slightly dizzy, almost queasy, as if the world had suddenly been tipped on its side. She reached out to steady herself, and a strange, loud *whoosh* seemed to envelop her.

Then everything was quiet.

She opened her eyes, but the room was dark. It was cold and damp, strange smells assailed her nostrils, pungent and rich, of spices and food and the scent of wet dogs.

As her eyes adjusted to the dimness, she heard the crackling of a fire.

Then someone coughed.

Immediately she whirled around. Across a vast room she saw a boy about her own age, wrapped in what appeared to be a very thick bathrobe with fur on the collar. On his head was an embroidered cap tied under his chin. He coughed again, a wracking hack that was painful to hear, as if it consumed his entire body.

Then he looked at her, raising his pale eyebrows. "I have been awaiting your visit." His voice was startlingly deep, his accent unusual.

Sam was about to ask him who he was, how she got there, when she recognized the boy.

He was Edward VI, the boy king of England. And he had been dead for almost five hundred years.

Chapter 2

Sam remained motionless on the wood plank floor, her mind searching frantically for an explanation of what she was seeing. Perhaps her father had grounded her for the rest of her life, and the shock of spending eternity in her bedroom caused her mind to snap. Maybe the harsh chemicals on her hair had done more than make her eyes water. This could very well be the first recorded case of perm-induced hallucination.

The most logical answer was that she had simply fallen asleep over her history book. Of course that was it. This was just a dream, although she had to admit she had outdone herself in the scenery department.

As her eyes adjusted, she realized the room was long but not terribly wide. There were elaborately carved wood panels covering the walls, intricate squares surrounded by spilling vines and what appeared to be grapes. The ceiling was high, with beautiful thick hammer-beams and molded plaster and scenes she couldn't make out in the shadows.

Even in her dream she was surprised there were no pictures on the walls. Instead there were several large tapestries. The one closest to her was of unicorns in a garden. There were no carpets on the floor, just more tapestries covering the tables.

The room seemed to move and shift with the flickering of burning thick, squat candles and the flames in the massive stone fireplace. The fireplace was so large she could have mistaken it for a door had there not been a fire roaring inside.

"Nice place," Sam said aloud to herself. After all, this was her dream and she could say whatever she wished. "I've never seen a walk-in fireplace before."

"What say you?" The dream-boy king asked.

"I said you have a very nice place." It was amusing, really, to have her imaginary character respond to her imaginary comments.

He just stared at her, and at that moment she realized he seemed every bit as startled to see her as she was to be there.

"My prayers have been answered," he said with awe. "So often I have prayed for you to come. And now you are here, and my faith is confirmed. This is most marvelous to our eyes."

Then he smiled.

It was a great smile, even with that silly hat he was wearing. His features were small but not as soft as they appeared in the painting. His nose was especially nice, very well shaped but with just the slightest upward turn at the tip. She couldn't see what color his eyes were, but they sparkled, and when he smiled they crinkled at the corners.

She decided if you have to dream, you might as well have a cute guy in it.

"This place is full of luxuries," he said. "But I am certain it cannot match the glory to which you are accustomed."

"Me?" Sam stood up, wondering briefly if her nightgown was transparent, then realizing it didn't matter. This was, after all, just a dream. "Nah. I mean, my house is nice and everything. But this is a mansion. My mom would go nuts to have this listing. She's a real estate agent, you know."

A large dog who had been sleeping next to the king shrugged to his paws and lumbered away, leaving only his wet fur scent and a few tufts of hair behind. Once again the king began to cough, and Sam stepped over to a long, tapestry-covered table, where a golden pitcher and several goblets were placed. The pitcher was filled with juice. There were also platters of fruit, two loaves of round bread, and a couple of hunks of very smelly cheese. She poured some of the juice into the goblet, crossed the room—feeling the cold floor under her bare feet—and passed it to the king.

Gratefully he accepted, and after swallowing some, handed the goblet back to her.

"I thank you," he rasped.

Up close he was even better looking than from across the room, but up close she could also see that he was a very sick guy. His complexion had an unnaturally pale cast, almost greenish. His eyes—dark brown, she could now see—were slightly swollen and red-rimmed. He took a deep breath and closed those too-bright eyes for a moment.

"Has my mother sent you?" His voice was suddenly weary, the thick exhaustion of a long illness. He seemed more like an elderly man than a young king. She wanted to reach out and touch him, but did not. This was only a dream, and her hand would probably pass right through him.

Then she stopped. How had she been able to pick up the pitcher and goblet if this was all a dream? And how could her feet feel the cold floor? The smells, the odor of the cheese and fruit, the fragrance of the fireplace and the overall dampness, like the musty scent of a long-folded shower curtain, still assailed her.

She looked down at the goblet, and decided to take a sip of juice, just to see if her sense of taste remained intact in this weird dream.

It was wine.

"Oh!"

Edward opened his eyes. "What is amiss?"

"This is wine." She pointed to the goblet.

"Yea. It is the best wine from France." Then he sat up. "Do you not have wine where you come from?"

"Sure we do. Just not until we're twenty-one."

His forehead creased in confusion as he leaned back in the large, dark wood chair. It looked uncomfortable, with sharp carvings of animals and what appeared to be dragons, with only a red velvet cushion on the seat to soften the effect. At the base of the chair were rods, so you couldn't tuck your feet under. You would be forced to sit straight, with your feet planted flat on the floor.

He didn't seem to mind the apparent discomfort. Instead he seemed troubled, as if in deep thought.

"What's bothering you?" Sam asked.

For a moment he didn't respond, and then he looked directly into her eyes.

Something fluttered in her stomach. It was so intense, the feeling she got from his gaze, the sharp intelligence she could almost touch. He looked as if the weight of the entire universe had been dropped on his shoulders.

"Does she forgive me?" She could barely hear him.

"Does who forgive you?"

"My mother." The words seemed to tear from his throat.

At first she weighed his meaning. What had he done? Sam knew that for whatever reason, whatever was happening to her in this weird dream, the answer was vital to the young king. Slowly she sat down cross-legged on the floor, just a few inches from the leg of his chair, and put down the goblet. She needed to think for a few seconds.

Then, suddenly, it all came to her with blinding clarity. Reaching up to feel the heavy silver necklace, she realized that her mother had forgiven her for creaming the BMW. She had been wrong, incredibly wrong, for taking the car with only her learner's permit and involving her best friend and her little brother. The outcome could have been much more disastrous than it had been. It was about the worst thing she could imagine.

Yet her mother had forgiven her.

If Sam's mother could forgive her for that, surely Edward's mother could forgive her son for whatever small infraction he had committed.

"Of course she forgives you," Sam said. She began to reach for his hand, and he stared down at her.

"No one ever touches me," he stated.

Quickly she drew away. Then she remembered reading something in a magazine about how you're never supposed to touch royalty, and she felt like a total jerk.

"But you may," he added, his voice was soft, gentle. She looked up at him, and he was smiling. "She forgives me? My mother?"

"Absolutely. Mothers always do." Sam swallowed, another strange fluttering rushing through her.

They sat for a long moment, and he just stared down at her, unblinking. She needed to think of something else to say, something to break the tension. "By the way, what did you do to make your mother angry?"

"I killed her. And later I had her two brothers beheaded."

Sam felt her jaw drop. Normally she would never do that in front of a cute guy she had just met, but this was an exception. Most cute guys don't confess to murder.

Why hadn't she read the chapter on the middle Tudors? It had been due last week, but as usual she had put it off to the last moment. She should have read it. Then she would have known what happened, what to say. Who had died and how. Instead she was absolutely clueless.

"Well," she said briskly, brushing her hands on her thighs with a confidence she didn't feel as she stood up. "I think I'm ready to wake up now."

"What mean you?"

"I mean I'm ready to go home now. This dream is over. Where are we, by the way?"

"Nonesuch."

"Nonesuch what?"

Edward rolled his eyes in a very unprincely fashion. "We are at the palace of Nonesuch. My father, the late king of glorious memory, built it, although he passed less than a fortnight within these walls. It was his favorite home, Nonesuch. He had to destroy a village or two to build it, but it was well worth it."

"That makes sense," Sam mumbled to herself. "This is a dream, so it doesn't exist. Nonesuch is a perfect name for the place." She then extended her hand. "Well, I'm waking up now. Good luck with everything. Hope you feel better soon."

Suddenly an explosive crash echoed through the room. Sam jumped and looked behind her.

A tall, slender man with deeply set, heavy-lidded eyes entered and left the huge doors swinging on their iron hinges. He wore a dark cape that flowed to his ankles, a high white collar that stood almost to his ears, and a strange black velvet hat that resembled a puffy black beret. His beard was pointed and flecked with gray, lending him a sinister appearance, at least to Sam. He was followed by six soldiers with sharp pikes, gleaming breastplates, and curved metal helmets with bright red plumes like those of Spanish conquistadors.

"Your Majesty," the man bowed. "We are here to arrest the assassin."

"The assassin?" Edward said in an imperious tone.

Sam, suddenly frightened but unsure of what or whom, looked around. "There's an assassin here?"

"You!" The man pointed an accusatory finger at Sam. "The guards heard voices from without. No one has been granted permission to approach the king's royal person. Thus the intruder must be apprehended and punished. Come with me, you traitor."

She forgot this was all a dream, that none of this was real and that she would soon wake up in her own bed. Sam was terrified.

"Leave us be," Edward proclaimed.

The man seemed surprised, and then uncertain. "But Your Majesty . . ."

"I said, leave us be! She is here by my command."

"I . . ."

"Shall I have the guards direct you, sir?" There was a cruel twist to Edward's voice, and Sam could see by the man's face that he heard it, too.

The imposing man shot her a look of pure venom, brief as it was potent and unmistakable.

"I apologize, Your Majesty. I was concerned for the safety of your person. I knew not that your visitor had been thus invited, that she was a . . . a guest."

"Leave, Northumberland. Leave at once."

The man lowered his eyes as if in submission, although Sam had a very good notion he was not someone to submit easily or often, and backed out of the room with more grace than seemed possible, as did the soldiers. The double doors closed quietly, and again they were alone.

A chill crept up her arms that had nothing to do with the room's temperature. She had a strong sense of being in over her head, of being thrust into a dangerous situation, but understanding none of it. Above all, she felt more alone than she had ever felt in her life.

This was no longer a dream. It had become a nightmare.

The room itself seemed sinister, the dark corners, the long shadows dancing with the shifting flames. Outside she could hear a shrill wind whistling, wheezing through the leaded windows, howling like a beast trying to enter.

"Who was that man?" Sam asked.

"That was the Duke of Northumberland, my protector and adviser. He assists me in ruling the kingdom."

"He assists? He doesn't seem like the assistant type."

Edward smiled. "You are observant. He

likes it not that I have been taking an active interest in political affairs. He wishes to rule by proxy, through me. But let us not speak of Northumberland. Let us speak of another."

"All right," Sam said hesitantly.

"Tell me," Edward began. "How does she fare?"

"How does who fare?"

"My mother. How does she fare?"

Sam forced herself to remain calm, even though he was asking about the mother he killed. The night was getting more bizarre by the minute. Since the chances of waking up anytime soon seemed increasingly remote, she decided the best course would be to play along, to roll with whatever punches came her way.

"Your mother? Oh, she's just fine."

"Did she send you to me?"

She thought for a moment. Was this a trick question? Was there a wrong or right answer? But then she looked at Edward's face, at the expression of hope there. And she was no longer quite so afraid. Whatever flashes of anger she had seen before were gone, vanished.

He wanted forgiveness.

She didn't need to fake her smile. "Yes, she

did send me here. And she forgives you for everything."

He seemed to savor her words and rose to his feet. Even as Sam stood in a strange place, in a world that may or may not even exist, she noticed that he was taller than she had realized, probably about six feet tall. Odd thing to notice at such a time.

"So I shall see her soon," he said with a nod.

Part of her knew she should just let it go, change the subject and start on her way home, wherever that was. Still, she was curious. How could he see his mother if he had killed her?

"You will see your mother soon?"

"Of course. And my father as well."

Sam had read far enough in the history book to know that Henry VIII, Edward's father, died when Edward was a small boy. That had been, after all, one of the multiple choice questions on the last test.

"I do know what is happening," he whispered. "You needn't pretend that I do not. You needn't protect me."

"Well," Sam began, stalling. Then she wondered if he really did know what this was all about, what was going on. "In that case, could you please tell me what is happening?"

"My sweet, sweet angel. I am dying, and you

have been sent to tell me so. And I suspect soon you will take me there."

Stunned, Sam could only stammer. "Where? Where will I take you?"

"Why, to heaven, of course." He reached up and touched one of her curls. "Fascinating. Do all angels have hair of such unnatural cast and texture?"

He thought she was an angel.

Before she could reply, he made one more comment.

"I bid you, keep a fair distance from candles and flames while you tarry on this earth."

"Excuse me?"

He thought she was an angel!

"I said, stay away from fire. Your hair will go up like a torch."

Chapter 3

Sam stood in front of the young King Edward, a guy who admitted to killing his mother and beheading two uncles, thought he himself was dying, and was operating under the misapprehension that she was an angel from heaven.

And she thought *she* was messed up.

Edward was still staring at her hair. "This is not of our earth," he proclaimed.

"No, it isn't," she stepped back. As she looked at him, a teenager like herself who seemed so very alive, she asked him a simple question. "Why do you think you are dying?"

His gaze shifted from her hair to her eyes, and she felt herself blush. They were standing so close she could feel his breath on her cheek.

"I will die for my sins," he stated plainly. "My illness is of a pernicious sort, and I am offered little hope."

"But you're too young to die." That seemed obvious, even to someone as confused as Edward.

"Do you jest? Or is the place from which you come so marvelous that the young are immune from the grasp of death?"

"Not entirely," she admitted. "But, yes, where I come from, well . . ." This was difficult to explain. "Where I come from, you are way too young to die."

"I am nearly sixteen."

"Really? So am I. When's your birthday?"

"October twelfth. When is yours?"

"Mine's April twentieth." Then Sam grinned. "I'm older than you are!"

"By a few months," he admitted. Then he, too, grinned. "But I am the undisputed king of England, Ireland, and France."

"I have my learner's permit," she countered, realizing that his king trumped her learner's permit. "Anyway, you're not going to die." Looking at him closely, however, she did see he didn't seem well. "Have you seen a doctor?"

"Ha! Every physician in the land has come to examine me, to poke and prod. I've been bled so many times, I . . . Here." He pushed up his right sleeve, the thick brocade of the robe stiff and unyielding. Under the robe was some sort of white shirt, with ties at his wrists. She was looking at the fabric, at the brilliant colored threads and the silken textures of his robe. But then she saw the crook of his arm, which was covered with welts and slashes, some clearly red with infection.

"Oh!"

"I usually say much worse than that," he examined them himself. "These blue ones are from the leeches."

"Leeches!"

"Yes, of course. They say it is the best way to cure consumption." He looked at her, his voice trailing off, peering closely at her face. "You have great beauty. Indeed that of an angel."

"Me?"

"No. I was speaking of Northumberland."

She glanced up from his arm, and he was smiling, a different glaze over his shining dark eyes now. Gradually the smile faded, and she recognized his expression. It was the same one Harry Walborsky had on his face right before he kissed her at Lori's Halloween party.

Then, abruptly, he pulled back and rolled down his sleeve.

"I bid you good night," he said, and walked

toward the door. The dog jumped up and followed his master.

Sam simply stood there, perplexed. "Um, excuse me?"

Edward turned, raising an eyebrow. "Yes?" He suddenly seemed about a million miles away.

"What about me?"

"I do not understand."

"Where will I sleep?"

That seemed to surprise him. "Can you not vanish as you came? I will speak to you on the morrow of my sins. So vanish."

Sam decided to ignore the unflattering implication of his request, which made her feel about as welcome as a used paper towel. "Well, no. I can't just vanish as I came."

"Why not?"

"Because," she began, stalling for as long as she could, hoping that something good would come to her. And it did. "Because, you see, while I am on the earth, I become a human. So I am unable to vanish until . . ."

An expression of dawning comprehension crossed his features. "I understand. You are on this earth, and thus act as we do while you walk among us." Then he smiled again, more at his own cleverness than at Sam's not vanishing. "That is why you could pour the wine, and why Northumberland frightened you. And why I could feel warmth when you were close to my person." Then it was his turn to blush before he continued. "For the duration of your visitation, you are a creature of this humanly world."

"Yes!" It had worked—he believed her.

Then a strange, disturbing thought came to her. What if he was right? Maybe she was an angel. Or a ghost. There had been a cable TV show on a couple of weeks before that said ghosts don't know they're dead, and that's why they haunt. Ghosts are simply dead people who don't know any better.

"What is wrong?" Gone was the remote teenage king, and once more he was just a nice guy, like someone you would sit next to in the school library who lends you a pen.

"What if I'm dead?" Sam blurted. "Oh my God. Maybe I'm dead, maybe I'm the ghost." It was all so hazy, what had happened. The sequence of events ran together like a terrible dream. "What if I killed everyone in my father's BMW?"

"Nay, you are not dead. You are an angel, a celestial being come down from the heavens to guide me."

She just looked at him. What else could she do? He had no idea what was going on, and neither did she. His notion was as logical as anything she could come up with at the moment.

"You are too young to die," he finally said.

At that the big dog lumbered over to Sam, his nails clicking on the floor, and began to wag his tail. She bent down to pat his head. At the same time Edward began to cough again, a hacking spasm that seemed to wrack his entire body.

Something clicked in Samantha's mind.

"You're allergic to fur!"

The dog kept on wagging his tail, Edward kept on coughing, and it all fell into place. "Oh my God, you're just like my little brother! Here," she grabbed the hound by his leather collar and pulled open the heavy door. Two guards appeared, pikes in hand. "Could you please take him away for a bit? We're experimenting."

They looked at Edward, who nodded through his cough.

"I mean, don't hurt him or anything," she eyed the sharp blades on the pikes, hesitating before letting them take the dog.

The guards exchanged perplexed glances,

and she handed the dog to the least intimidating-looking one. Then she turned back to Edward, whose coughing fit was beginning to subside. "Okay, now we need to vacuum this place to get out all the fur balls and . . ."

"Vacuum? We need to make the palace a void?"

"Sorry, I mean sweep. We need to sweep and . . ."

He looked absolutely exhausted. And ill. Sam took a deep breath. "Maybe we can do this all tomorrow."

Edward shook his head. "The events of this evening have left me befuddled. I bid you good night."

"I still don't have anyplace to sleep."

Edward thought for a moment. "It would be unseemly for you to share my chamber, would it not?"

"It would. Coed sleepovers are usually frowned upon."

Edward looked at her with an expression she was beginning to recognize as "huh?" Then he brightened. "I have the solution! You shall sleep with my cousin Jane."

"Cousin Jane?"

"Yea, she is here in this very palace, arrived this afternoon from her family home. You will enjoy her company. Some find her too somber, but not I. She is learned, perhaps the most scholarly female in the entire realm. And she is most fascinating on the topic of religion. Why, as an angel you should find her theories of great interest."

Great, Sam thought. Edward's cousin Jane, the family genius. She's sure to be loads of fun.

He gestured for her to follow him out of the room, and she did so, keenly aware as she stepped into the hallway that she was wearing nothing but her nightgown, her new necklace, the bad perm and even worse dye job. Guards snapped to attention.

Sam assumed Edward would take her to his cousin. Instead he instructed the guards to lead her to Lady Jane's chamber, and then he turned to the right through a door with a big brass knob in the center. There was no good night, no other such nicety.

Then she was alone with the guards. She felt just like the dog she had banished from the room a few moments earlier, a creature to be led away by the collar.

The guards were silent as they escorted the king's guest through the corridors. She walked stiffly, very aware that she was barefoot. The guards made no attempt at conversation, which was just fine with Sam, who had no desire to make small talk with two massive men with sharpened pikes. Part of her wanted to know where they were going, the other part was simply delighted they didn't ask any questions.

As dark as the room had been, the hallways were even dimmer, with only torches placed intermittently along the walls, casting uneven light. On the other wall were vast closed windows, the views outside obscured by the pitch black night, further distorted by brushed glass divided into diamond shapes with ribbons of lead.

At last, after ducking into winding back staircases and through yet more hallways, they led her to a closed door. Knocking once, the guard with the scar spoke for the first time.

"Lady Jane? The king has sent forth a guest for your pleasure."

Sam almost corrected him, since she wasn't there for Lady Jane's pleasure, but because the king didn't know what else to do with her. She remained silent, though.

He knocked again and without waiting for an answer, he pushed open the door.

Sam was mortified, wondering what Lady Jane would think of her, this stranger bursting in on her in the middle of the night. But the open door revealed a girl about her own age, under the thick, plush covers of a richly carved canopy bed, a book in her hands and several candles on her bedside table. The candles were of various heights, dripping great globs of wax on the table, the flames bending with the draft from the open door.

Lady Jane didn't act the least bit upset or even surprised, the way Sam reacted when her little brother barged in every few minutes. Sam smiled at the girl before her. Lady Jane easily could have been one of her own friends reading a paperback novel in bed.

"I'm sorry to disturb you, Lady Jane, but . . ." Before Sam could continue, the two guards clicked their heels and marched away. Sam immediately looked down at the floor, wondering what would happen next. Nothing did. Cautiously, she glanced up.

Looking over at Jane, she thought she saw the briefest flicker of a smile, but then it was gone. For some reason Sam was taken aback at how pretty Jane was, even in the shadows and with a rather silly lace cap on her head. Her first impression was of thick, wavy red hair flowing over the girl's shoulders and covering her blankets and pillows. Her complexion seemed luminous, but perhaps it was the candlelight, which Sam's mother always insisted was flattering to everyone.

Whatever the lighting, Jane's features were lovely. She seemed to have the same sparkling brown eyes as Edward, but her nose was smaller, her face more oval and her lips fuller than his. She reminded Sam of an actress on a new teen television show, an all-American cheerleader type.

Without saying anything, Jane pulled back the covers on the other side of the bed, as if offering Sam space, then went back to reading her book. Sam also realized that Lady Jane was incredibly tiny, even smaller than Jason.

Standing in the doorway, feeling awkward and more than a little embarrassed, Sam was at a loss as to what she should do next. Was she supposed to jump into the bed with some strange girl? The room was quite little, so she could see there wasn't another bed there, just a rounded chest that looked like it belonged to a pirate and a couple of stiff, uncomfortable-looking chairs.

"Um, where should I sleep?"

Lady Jane didn't seem to hear her, so intent was she on her book. She frowned for a moment, as if puzzled by a passage, her lips moving silently as she read it once again. Then her eyebrows arched in understanding, and she turned the page.

If anything was amiss on Lady Jane's face, Sam decided, it was her eyebrows. They were very light, almost invisible, giving her a slightly surprised expression.

Sam shifted her weight from one bare, cold foot to the other, and cleared her throat once. Then another time. Finally she cleared her throat so loudly she thought the windows would rattle.

Lady Jane looked up from her book. "Yes?"

"Um, where should I sleep?" Sam asked, feeling totally lame.

"There is space beside me." She stared at Sam for a few seconds, then returned to the book.

Sam remained where she stood. "Excuse me?"

This time Lady Jane looked up right away. "Yes?"

"What are you reading?"

Jane blinked. "*Phaedon Platonis.* Have you read it?" She seemed eager.

"I'm not sure. Who wrote it?"

"Plato." Jane sighed, shaking her head slightly as she focused once more on her book.

"Excuse me," Sam hated to disturb her again, but it was necessary. "Where's the bathroom?"

Jane gave Sam a blank stare. "You require a bath?"

"No, I just need to use the bathroom, if you know what I mean. And maybe brush my teeth."

Now Jane put her book down. "You have teeth that have hair on them?"

"Not really. It just feels like it sometimes." As she spoke Sam suddenly realized two things. One, they didn't have bathrooms back then. She would have to wait about four centuries for that. And two, they didn't brush their teeth.

The one thing in her history book that had made an impression was the paragraph on Tudor hygiene. Or, more accurately, the lack of it. Although it wasn't on the last test (nothing she ever knew was), she remembered reading they occasionally rubbed their teeth with cloths, or gave gold toothpicks as special gifts.

That went a long way in explaining the darkened sneers of the guards.

For the first time, Jane seemed interested in Sam. "Where are you from? Your manner of speech is most extraordinary."

Sam thought for a moment. "I'm from a distant land far, far away." She tried to sound mystical enough to satisfy Jane, but it didn't work.

"What is the name of it? I do know my geography." Then she cocked her head slightly. "And how is it that you have become acquainted with my cousin the king?"

"Ah, that is a long story." It really wasn't, she thought to herself. But she was hoping Jane would drop the topic.

"I am ever so fond of a good story," Jane enthused. "Pray, do tell me."

Sam interrupted. "I have a question!"

"Yes?"

She tried to think of something that would get the persistent Lady Jane on to something else, divert her toward less uncertain territory. Then it came to her.

"My question is about your cousin the king," she began. Jane nodded for her to continue. "He told me he killed his mother and two of his uncles. He seems like such a nice person. I really can't imagine him doing something so terrible."

"He sayeth such a thing?" Jane was genuinely surprised. Then she looked at Sam. "Here, climb into the bed. This April night is chill, and the floor is cold."

She was right. It was cold. Sam also realized it was April in this place, just as it had been April back at home. Somehow, that was something of a relief.

The bed was warm, if not quite as soft and comfortable as it looked. Some of the pillows were a little on the hard side, especially the round bolsters. Still, the blankets felt wonderful, especially on her feet.

"Are you aware of the history of our king?" Jane asked.

"No. I'm supposed to be, but I never read the chapters that were assigned and . . ." Jane was looking at her quizzically, so Sam simplified her answer. "No."

"How curious. I marvel that one can be ignorant of such recent and vital events."

"I guess it does seem odd." Sam shrugged. "But have you ever gone someplace new? I mean, have you ever traveled to a place you had never been before, and not known what everyone else seemed to know? It makes you feel pretty stupid."

A slow smile spread over Jane's face. "Yea, that has happened to me, and in this very place. I myself knew nothing of the ways of the court until I came here. And the only reason I was able to learn the custom was because I was taught. It is not easy to be a stranger, is it?"

Sam shook her head.

"Then I shall teach you. Now, my cousin Edward is the king. His father was the late King Henry of marvelous glory. His mother was Jane Seymour. She was his third wife, you know."

"He had eight wives, right?"

"No. Only six. Because he was Henry the Eighth, it does get a bit confusing. Well, the good Queen Jane died soon after Edward's birth. That is what I believe Edward means when he says he killed her. He feels his birth caused his mother's death."

"Oh, I see," Sam said. "He made it sound as if he killed her on purpose."

"Of course not! He must feel guilt that she died bringing him into this world. Be that as it may, the story continues. Queen Jane had two brothers, Edward's uncles. The youngest uncle was Thomas, wild and dashing and said to be the most handsome man at court."

"Was he?"

"I never thought him as such. He held too high an opinion of his own charms."

"Ah." Sam nodded. "He was in love with himself."

"Yea! Now, at the time the great King Henry died, I was already at court, having been sent there by my parents to be taught under the guardianship of Queen Catherine, the king's last wife."

"What happened to Queen Catherine after King Henry died?"

"She married her one true love. Thomas Seymour, Queen Jane's brother and Edward's uncle. Catherine died in childbed, and soon after their infant daughter died as well."

"How sad."

"Yes, well, after Catherine died Edward could not rule on his own. He was only nine years old. So there was need for a protector to guide him. Thomas felt that job should be his, but so did his older brother Edward. Both were the new king's uncles.

"So what happened?"

"Edward Seymour, Duke of Somerset, took over the role of protector. Somerset, unlike Thomas, was a sober, deliberate man. He felt he should be the only protector. And I believe he did have the best interests of both his nephew and the country at heart."

"What did the young King Edward wish?"

Jane shrugged. "That made little difference,

as he was but a small boy. He loved his older uncle Somerset, but feared his strictness. But all agreed that Somerset was the best choice for protector.

"Somerset did use his new influence at court to keep his younger brother Thomas away from Edward. Thomas was virtually banished from the halls. But Thomas was always rash and always quick to anger. One day he broke into the king's chambers to tell him of his desire to be protector, hoping to tell him how much more fun that would be. But he was captured. And since it is considered high treason to get close to the king without permission from the king or his protector, Thomas was beheaded as a would-be assassin."

Sam shuddered, realizing that is the exact crime of which she was unintentionally guilty—breaking into the king's rooms unannounced. No wonder the guy in the cape had been so upset!

"How did your cousin Edward feel about all of this?"

"He was torn, for he loved his uncle Thomas. But Thomas had gone too far and committed treason. Edward knew that well. And for the crime of treason Thomas was executed."

"But the young king had no choice. He did

not behead his uncle." Sam was beginning to understand.

"Nay. It was the protector who pressed the charges and had his own brother put to death."

"So then there was only Somerset. Where is he now?"

"He was never able to regain the trust of the court. He was feared and disliked. After all, if a man is capable of ordering his own brother's death, is there anything of which he is not capable? So the duke of Somerset was eventually toppled, forced from office and beheaded for treason. In his place came another man, John Dudley, the duke of Northumberland." Jane shuddered at the mere mention of the man's name.

"I met him! He thought I was an assassin!"

"That would indeed be Northumberland. But I beg of you, do not cross him. He is not to be held in light regard."

"Now this all makes more sense. But why does Edward feel as if it's his fault that his uncles were beheaded? His one uncle had the other executed, and then it sounds as if Northumberland did the same to Somerset. Edward had no choice in the matter. So he believes he's to blame for three deaths, but he really isn't."

"You are right. But he takes things to heart. At times I think perhaps that he is too kind to be king. Other times, though . . ." Jane stopped herself.

"You may be right," Sam said, thinking of the young man and his sad eyes.

Jane shook her head, then sighed. "I grow weary."

"Me, too." Sam didn't know how to ask one more question. "Um, Lady Jane?"

"Yes," her voice was suddenly tired.

"Where may I, eh . . . relieve myself?"

"Oh. There is a chamber pot in the corner, under that large chair—just behind the small velvet curtain."

"Thank you," Sam answered uncertainly.

"May I ask you a question?" Jane said.

Sam nodded.

"What is your name?"

Sam smiled. In all of the hours she had been there, not a single person had asked her name. "My name is Samantha McKenna, but everyone calls me Sam."

"Sam? That is an unusual name for a female." Jane smiled, revealing very small white teeth. And up close she had freckles, lots of tiny reddish freckles.

Suddenly she realized she liked Lady Jane a

great deal. "Yep, my name is Sam. Just Sam."

"Very well." Jane snuffed out the candles with her fingers, so all that remained was a pitch dark room and the lingering scent of wax and flame. "Good night, just Sam."

"Good night, Lady Jane."

In the blackness of night, with no street lamps or car headlights or sounds of planes flying overhead, with only the soft sounds of Lady Jane's breathing, she wondered what would happen next.

Then she fell asleep.

Chapter 4

Sam sighed and rolled over in her sleep, a slight smile on her face as she recalled the dream she'd had. That had to have been the wildest dream in history! Even half awake she caught the sheer entertainment value of her own thoughts—a historically amazing dream about the events of history. About the middle Tudors, about kings and queens and beheadings and . . .

Her test!

With a jolt she sat upright, her mind muddled by confusion and sleep. The big history test was this morning!

Then she stopped.

The room was momentarily unfamiliar, the bed oddly large, a four-poster antique with a red brocade canopy and heavy curtains partially closed like the flaps of a tent. The brocade matched the curtain under the chair across the room, the one with the chamber pot beneath. Instinctively she clutched the blanket to her chin and felt the weight of her new locket, the one her mother had given her as an early sixteenth birthday gift.

What was happening? Why was she still there? How come she hadn't managed to wake up yet?

The room looked completely different in the morning sun, far less forbidding and far more welcoming. The windows allowed light to flood every corner with warmth. Birds were singing outside. An expanse of lush green was visible in the distance, beyond fanciful-looking turrets and towers, some with triangular flags flapping in the wind. It resembled a theme park, a place where no expense had been spared on detail and quality materials. All that was lacking was a much needed tour guide to let her know where she was and when she could leave.

She wondered if it was spring here, too, in this fantasy theme park. Just yesterday, back home, it had been April.

Was it spring here, wherever she was?

There were sounds outside the room, in the hallway, conversations muted by the heavy door, footsteps passing by without pausing.

Sam had no idea what time it was, since the only things on the bedside table—where a clock would usually be—were the candles she recalled from last night, now cold, with thick drips of wax and blackened wicks. There was no clock in the room.

Clothes had been neatly laid out on the other side of the bed, where Lady Jane had been the night before. The clothes were peculiar, all in pieces, sleeves and a skirt and a quilted bodice. Only the sleeves, which were black velvet, were of the same color, although one sleeve had white laces up the side, the other had red ones. The full skirt was a deep green and the bodice was light gray. A little cap made of plain linen was off to the side, the only thing she could clearly identify. There was a stiff piece of beige canvas with laces crisscrossing on one side, and Sam held it up, as if its purpose would suddenly become apparent if she examined it from all angles.

The more she looked at the bits of fabric—the sleeves and skirt pieces in such an odd assortment of colors—the more they resembled a partially completed home economics project. A horrible thought crossed her mind: What if she was supposed to sew this dress together? And if she did a lousy job, would she be beheaded?

It seemed absurd. But then, the very fact that she was still smack in the middle of sixteenth-century England was about as absurd as it gets. She held a sleeve along her arm, wondering if they had glue back then.

She'd taken home economics the previous semester. What she had done to the one dress she attempted to make was similar to what she had done to her father's BMW.

There was a single knock on the door before it was opened. Lady Jane entered hesitantly, a strange expression on her lovely face. Sam was momentarily taken aback by how very tiny she was, not simply short, but overall tiny. Her waist couldn't be more than twenty inches around, probably a lot less.

She wore a full-length gown of rich maroon, with a deep, square neckline. A bit of white material was gathered at the collar and cuffs. The sleeves were puffed from the shoulders to the elbows, then almost impossibly tight to the wrists. Covering her hair was a rounded headdress, with rows of tiny pearls along the border. Just a little of her red hair, parted in the middle, was visible. In the back was a flowing black velvet veil hanging past her small waist.

But the most striking aspect to her outfit was the peculiar shape of the skirt, puffed out all around as if she had dozens of petticoats underneath.

The clothing made her seem older than she had the night before, stiffer, not like the girl in a loose nightgown reading a favorite book by candlelight. Now she looked like the formal portraits in Sam's history book. Now Lady Jane *looked* like history itself, prim and remote.

"I did not wish to wake you this morning," Jane said. "Here, I have procured a gable hood from the royal wardrobe," she held up a triangular headdress that looked like a miniature A-frame house. "And shoes. And hose."

In her other hand was what appeared to be some sort of canvas birdcage. "Here's a Spanish farthingale."

Sam was about to point out that the farthingale, obviously a bird, had escaped. There was no bottom on the cage. But she didn't want to alarm Jane, who already seemed ill at ease.

"Oh. Thank you," Sam said as she slid out of bed and took the hose, which were two limp-looking, leg-shaped, cream-colored things with thick seams and stiff ruffles on the tops. She stared at them, vaguely surprised that she could ever long for a pair of panty hose.

The dark blue shoes were more like leather slippers, low heeled and slashed at the sides. It was impossible to tell the left from the right. They were too delicate to last even a day at the shopping mall—her mother would declare them flimsy and impractical. The headdress had small metal clips on the inside to hold it in place, and Sam had a sudden image of wearing a birdhouse on her head.

Struggling for something to say, Sam thought of a hundred light comments, mostly about the weather being too warm for hats and long sleeves, but she remained silent. There was definitely something up with Lady Jane. She was so different from the night before, standoffish, not even a hint of a smile. It was more than just the clothes. She wouldn't even look Sam directly in the eyes, her gaze darting around the room with obvious unease.

Was she even four and a half feet tall? Sam wondered.

"I had a conversation with my cousin," Jane began. "We were at chapel this morning. I thought it best to allow you to sleep, Sam." She pronounced her name awkwardly, the way an exchange student from France would.

"You saw the king? How is he feeling this morning?"

"He fares well," she replied tentatively.

"I know his cough sounds terrible, but I really think he just has allergies. Probably to dogs and fur and all that. Maybe to wheat and nuts as well. He should really be checked out for all that."

"Checked out?"

"Yes. By doctors . . . physicians."

Jane remained quiet for a moment, then spoke in a neutral tone. "The physicians have said he suffers from consumption. That is a universal agreement."

Consumption, Sam thought. Why did that sound so familiar? Wasn't there a movie or book with a character who died of consumption? Whatever it was, it didn't sound good.

"What are the symptoms of consumption?" Sam asked. "I mean, is it from something you eat?"

For some reason, Sam's simple question totally freaked out Lady Jane. Her small, freckled hand covered her mouth, her dark brown eyes grew wide and round.

"Lady Jane, what's wrong?"

She just shook her head.

"Did I say something wrong?"

Jane remained still, then drew her hand away. "Nay. It was you and Edward."

"The king?"

"He told me that he believes you are not a creature of our earth."

"Oh." She took a deep breath.

"Is this true?"

Sam chewed her bottom lip. She had no one else to trust. Things couldn't possibly get any weirder. It was as if she had nothing to lose.

"I don't know," Sam admitted, putting the clothing Jane had given her on the bed next to the other things. "I honestly don't know exactly what's going on. All I know is that I'm not from here, I didn't grow up in this place. Everything is strange and unfamiliar."

Suddenly Sam had an overwhelming desire to cry, a fierce urge more powerful than sobbing on the first night of sleep-away camp. She was utterly alone in this world, alone with only her memories and identity. There was nothing she could do or say to make anything different.

"I don't know." The words tore from her throat. "Oh, Jane, please believe what I am about to tell you."

Jane clutched the bedpost and nodded for her to continue.

Sam took a deep breath. "Okay, here goes. Yesterday afternoon, at least it was yesterday for me, I was at my own home, in Winnetka, Illinois. That's in the United States of America."

"The Americas?" Jane's voice was a bare whisper. "But there is scarce a civilized person in the Americas."

"Well, where I come from—*when* I come from, I should say, it is called the United States of America. And it's very civilized. We're a nation, a democracy. So is England by then. Wait a minute—what year is this?"

"It is the Year of Our Lord 1553."

The magnitude, the absolute, undeniable reality of the situation was staggering. Hearing Jane state the truth so simply, so clearly, stating it as irrefutable fact, was like a splash of ice water on her face.

This *was* real. It was no dream.

Sam sat on the edge of the bed, her knees weak, and rubbed her eyes before continuing. "So yesterday I was at home, with my little brother and my best friend, Lori."

"Lori?"

Sam smiled for the first time, her real smile. "Yep, Lori. And my little brother is named Jason. So it was Lori's idea to do this to my hair. It was supposed to be blond and curly, not stiff and ugly. My sixteenth birthday is coming up, and I'm having a big party. She thought we could lighten and curl my hair for the party and . . ."

Suddenly she stopped. Why was she telling this to Lady Jane, a girl who read Plato and didn't seem to give a hoot about fashion and hair and sweet sixteen parties?

This was a girl who lived over four hundred years before Sam was born.

Jane glanced down, her expression unreadable from under her headdress.

"Anyway," Sam proceeded, "I got into trouble. I broke something important to my father, who was away on a business trip. I mean, this was his favorite thing that I broke. He came home that night, a few hours after this happened"—she pulled up a piece of her hair. "I knew I was in major trouble. My dad would absolutely kill me. I was in my room, my chamber," she corrected. "I was sitting there on my bed one moment reading my history book. Next minute, zap! I was there in Edward's private chamber, in my nightgown."

Jane said nothing. Instead she walked to the fireplace and rested her hand on the mantel, clicking a gold ring against the stone as if in thought.

"Lady Jane," Sam stated clearly. "I have come here from the future, from almost five hundred years from now. I don't know how this happened. You may not believe me, but it's the absolute truth."

Jane remained silent.

So many things crossed Sam's mind during those long moments. That Jane would accuse her of witchcraft. That she would be charged with treason for appearing at court without any connections. That this admission could very well spell the end of her life.

Strangely, though, no matter the outcome, the immediate result was a sense of pure relief, just to tell someone the absolute truth.

Jane turned to Sam. "I dare say, your story is most fantastic."

"Do you mean 'fantastic' as in good? Or 'fantastic' as in unbelievable?"

"Both, I fancy."

"Do you believe me?" Sam had to know the answer.

Again Jane tapped her ring against the stone mantel, a hypnotic sound that seemed to imitate the ticking of a clock that was not there. Then she turned to Sam. "I read of strange things, of magic and sorcery. Yet I have never before seen the results of such extraordinary events. That does not mean they are untrue."

She seemed to weigh her own words before she spoke again. "This defies all logic. It is a fearsome concept, that you journeyed from a place so far away in both years and miles. Yet, Sam, your tale has the sound of truth." Jane's voice dropped to a whisper. "You sayeth you fear your father?"

Sam nodded. "Not all the time. Just when I do something wrong."

"Does he use you ill physically?"

Sam was confused. "What do you mean?"

"Does he whip you and beat you?"

"No! Of course not!" She was genuinely shocked. "Does your father ever hit you?"

"Only when I am guilty of a transgression," she said softly. "But often the transgression is in his mind, or in that of my mother's. Then I am beaten with a whip, or a flayed stick."

"How awful." Sam looked at Jane differently now. The poor girl, to have parents who hurt her.

"That is why I wished to be with Queen Catherine, and now to be here, away from them. I can study here with my tutor, Master

Elmer. He is kind and gentle, as is my cousin Edward. He protects me, for even my parents have no authority over the king. Maybe that is why you are here, too. To be safe from your parents. Perhaps God has sent you here for that reason."

"It really wasn't that bad. They were just going to ground me or something."

"Grind you!" Jane almost shouted. "Heavens! Barbaric! They would grind you!"

"No! No, not grind me up. They would ground me, which means they would make me stay inside after school."

Jane blinked. "That would be your punishment?"

Sam nodded.

"You would not be beaten? Not even a little?"

"No. They have laws against that where I come from. And besides, my parents would never hit me. Never."

"Then there must be some other reason for you to be here. Perhaps a divine mission." Then she brightened. "Perhaps you are here to help my cousin regain his health. I did take note of his cheer. It has been many long months since I have seen him in such marvelous spirits as this morning."

Sam was almost afraid to press further. "I don't know how or why this happened. I mean, I'm just a regular kid back home."

"A 'kid'?" Jane seemed startled.

"Yeah. A teenager, a soon-to-be adult. Someone who is almost trusted as a competent human being. Whatever."

Finally Jane smiled. "A kid. I thought you meant in your time, you are a kid—a baby goat."

Now it was Sam's turn to be surprised. "A goat?"

"Well," she said and looked down, her face turning red as if trying to keep from laughing. "It would indeed explain your hair."

A sudden warm rush swept over Sam, the wonderful, familiar feeling of being with a friend. Jane glanced up, her dark eyes meeting Sam's, a distinct twinkle lighting her features.

"You believe me," Sam stated.

Jane nodded. "No one would go willingly to court in a nightgown and goat hair."

Suddenly Sam was unable to speak. Here she was in a foreign place, and this kind royal cousin believed the most unbelievable of stories. Her throat tightened as if she had swallowed an orange.

Jane reached for Sam's hand. "I will be your

tutor," she said. "Just as Queen Catherine showed me the ways of the court, I will show you. Follow me, and you will soon become familiar with the customs here." Jane straightened, a no-nonsense air as she briskly stepped over to the clothing on the bed. "I will be your ladies' maid this morning as well as your tutor. Have you attire such as this in your . . . place?"

Sam shook her head, and without hesitation Jane began the long process of getting Sam dressed.

The first of many surprises was that Sam was expected to wear her nightgown under all of the clothing. As weird as that was, it wasn't nearly as bizarre as the canvas thing, which Sam quickly learned was a corset. Petticoats laced onto the bottom of the corset, as did the loose birdcage. A Spanish farthingale, it seemed, wasn't a bird but a hoop skirt thing. Next came the kirtle, which was what Jane called the skirt. Then a square-necked bodice was laced in the back. Jane tied the sleeves onto the bodice, explaining as she worked that those plain sleeves could be exchanged for others, or a fancier bodice could be used with the same sleeves.

The hose tied at her upper thighs, and Jane made Sam adjust them for comfort.

Her nimble fingers seemed to fly, and Sam just listened to Jane's soothing voice, to her accent and the way she used words.

At one point she stopped to look at Sam and said that she, too, had sometimes felt very "alonely."

Then she continued, and soon Sam was dressed, including the heavy headpiece that covered her hair and the lappets—which were like a long veil—tucked in the back. The plain linen cap was worn under the headdress, and Sam secretly wished she had a round headdress like Jane's instead of the little house.

"There," Jane said with approval. "Now you are a proper lady."

Sam looked down at her own body, all bound in what seemed like an instrument of torture of various colors. And she did, indeed, look just like one of those paintings, although she couldn't recall seeing an outfit quite like this one. Jane had said that she had not wished to arouse suspicion by gathering an entire outfit from one source, leaving Sam to wonder if she had simply stolen bits and pieces of clothing from many women rather than one costume from a single person.

Although each piece was smaller than what Sam had thought she could possibly squeeze into, by tying the various laces more loosely, it all seemed to fit. The skirt was a few inches off the ground, so Jane told her to bend her knees a bit and no one would notice.

Jane seemed pleased with the results, and Sam supposed she should be pleased as well. At least from what she could tell—there was no mirror in Lady Jane's chamber. No clock, no mirror. No television or telephone or blow dryer or mascara. Sam had actually dressed without the benefit of a refreshing shower, minty toothpaste, or even clean clothes.

A thought crossed her mind. Who had worn these clothes before her?

She swallowed, remembering the long list of Tower of London victims from her history book. She had been just about to read the names when she came here.

"Are you ready to face the court?"

Sam nodded. *Court.* It sounded as if she was about to go on trial. In a very real way, she was.

Sam had been so intent on simply maneuvering in the torture chamber called clothing that she had momentarily forgotten their destination. The corset alone was like slipping into a small iron pipe, the shoes were way too small and her pinkie toes were already beginning to bulge out the sides of the soft leather, and she was in constant fear of the hose rolling to the floor and tripping her up.

The farthingale made her feel like a giant Liberty Bell, swaying from side to side as she walked, although she quickly discovered that by keeping her hips as still as possible, she could minimize the effect.

The headdress was another matter. It felt like a vise and must have looked like, well, a birdhouse. Or a barn. Of course she had no clue, since there were apparently no mirrors in sixteenth-century England. Perhaps that was for the best, she thought, as she reached up to scratch under the headdress. She did know that it reached almost to her shoulders, and that the only good thing about it was that her hair was completely hidden.

Jane cleared her throat as they walked, giving a disapproving shake of her head when Sam scratched or twitched. Sam paid no attention to their route. Her arms itched from within the confines of the sausage-casing sleeves, and every time she tugged at her sleeve or tried to loosen the bodice, Lady Jane elbowed her and frowned. When she reached down to pull up her droopy hose, Jane whispered, "Behave!"

Then they were in the doorway of a large room filled with what seemed like hundreds of people.

Sam froze. Jane nodded for her to proceed. At least that is what Sam thought Jane had meant. They both began to enter the threshold together.

Unfortunately Sam had miscalculated both the width of the doorway and the even more extreme width of their skirts. She had the same problem parking a car—depth perception, her driver's ed instructor had called it. Anyway, the result of the dueling farthingales was that both Lady Jane and Sam became momentarily wedged in the doorway—with the entire court watching.

"Back away," Jane hissed.

"I can't," Sam shot back. "Let me go through first."

"You may not. Unless you are a duchess, princess or queen, my rank is greater than yours! Therefore I proceed you."

"But I'm stuck!"

By this time everyone had turned toward them, all conversation stopped. With a shove of surprising strength, Jane sent Sam flying backward. Almost unbelievably, Sam managed to avoid landing on her rear end and only staggered a few feet before being caught by a guard.

Jane, her composure regained, entered the hallway with regal posture, then turned to Sam, who followed somewhat less gracefully, whacking her skirt on both sides of the doorway as she walked.

There was pure silence as the courtiers stared, blatant curiosity on their faces.

What faces they were. Faces such as Sam had never seen.

For a moment her very breath was knocked from her body. Before then she had only gazed at Edward, a few guards, Northumberland and Lady Jane. Now she was confronted with the people of 1553, the humanity that had composed the world of that time.

Of this time, she corrected herself.

Somehow, the very face of humanity had changed. These people were raw, almost naked in their expressions. The texture of their complexions was rough and unaided by cosmetics or treatments of any sort. Childhood illnesses, accidents, vivid birthmarks were all visible. To her left was a young man with a huge mole on his cheek—the sort of thing that was routinely removed in a doctor's office in Sam's time. An otherwise elegant lady smiled at Lady Jane, exposing a set of not-quite-full greenish teeth.

In fact no one had white teeth. As they stepped farther into the hall, Sam realized that no one was quite clean either. The stench of unwashed bodies was almost unbearable, even though it wasn't a particularly warm day. It wasn't just the mild smell you get when someone next to you raises a hand in summer school. This was the result of layers of odor, days and weeks and even months of nastiness imbedded into velvet that had never been washed. As they passed through the room, Sam noticed that none of the courtiers were as elegant up close as at a distance.

Besides their green teeth and overall unwashed state, the people wore clothing that was stained. A man who bowed low at the waist to Lady Jane had a big glob of something down the front of his doublet. All the skirts were streaked. The men's hose drooped, much as she knew her own did. Headdresses were askew. They were all a mess.

Also they were all quite short! Most of the women were about five feet tall, Sam guessed, and the men were not much taller. Sam towered over them. It was almost like stepping into a classroom of first graders—she felt like an absolute giant.

Even with their stains and short stature, their clothing was still rich and luxurious, with fur and flashes of jewels and yards of velvet. There wasn't a bare head in the lot, everyone wore a hat, which did make them all seem a bit taller. The men wore velvet puffy things or cocked berets studded with dangling pearls or feathers. The women wore headdresses, some like Sam's, but most were the rounded kind—French hoods, Jane had called them.

Sam desperately wanted to trade in her birdhouse for a French hood. Plus it did not escape her notice that no one else was wearing a dress made of a half dozen different colors. That thought made her grin.

"What is amiss?" Jane whispered as they entered the hall.

"I have just experienced my first medieval fashion crisis."

"Pardon me?"

"Never mind," Sam swallowed.

They were incredible, these people. Had she seen some of them in, say, a shopping mall or at a fast-food joint, she would have averted her eyes out of politeness. They were so imperfect, so very dirty. There were men with scars disfiguring their features, ladies with facial hair, crossed eyes and pockmarks. Of course some were lovely, like Lady Jane, or handsome, like Edward, who wasn't there at the moment.

Still, these were real people, and the realness of them made Sam feel humble, even embarrassed.

How many times had she judged people by their appearances? And now here she was, being judged for the very same reason. She was lucky enough to have Lady Jane at her side, a royal cousin.

What if she had entered alone?

As they walked through the room, the crowds parting and Jane nodding gracefully, Sam caught a whiff of another fragrance. It was heavenly, sublime. It wafted over her like a cloud of pure joy. It tickled her nose. It gladdened her very being.

It was food.

Lady Jane was introducing her to a group of men who seemed very eager to please Lady Jane, but all Sam could do was nod and look in the direction of the food. The men bowed, and Sam responded with a distracted half bow of her own.

The food was just a few yards away.

"I'm starving," she blurted out. Her hunger was all that mattered to Sam right then.

"Sam . . ." Jane began.

"Forgive me, Lady Jane. I haven't eaten in over four hundred years."

Jane was still speaking as Sam headed toward the buffet. And what a spread it was! There were lattice-topped pies and fruit of all kinds. There were massive hunks of cheese with crusty loaves of bread, pitchers of wine and ale, all garnished with leaves and flowers and . . . feet.

"Ugh!" She recoiled in spite of her hunger. There were clenched talons—complete with toenails—on the roast chicken!

"Is my lady displeased?" A male voice whispered in her ear. She turned toward the voice, her headdress tipping as she moved.

There he was. The duke of Northumberland.

Chapter 5

Remain calm, Sam urged herself, forgetting all about her hunger.

"I repeat, does something displease you?" In daylight the Duke of Northumberland was actually quite handsome, and a lot younger than he had appeared the night before. His face was still unlined, the beard just beginning to show flecks of gray mingled in the deep brown. His eyes were a piercing dark blue, almost black, and his eyelashes were surprisingly lush. He was good-looking in a Shakespearean-actor way, the type of man her mom would find cool in a coffee commercial.

"No, sir," she replied, clasping her hands before her as if she had just been caught digging into the cookie jar. It crossed her mind that "sir" was probably not the right thing to call a duke, but then in Illinois she had been introduced to very few dukes. For that matter, her encounters with kings and titled ladies had been quite limited as well.

The duke was still speaking.

"The repast is for all to enjoy, including you, our most attractive and mysterious visitor. May I assist?"

"I . . ." she began.

Without waiting for her answer he took a silver plate and motioned for her to follow. "A little fruit, perhaps? Some sweetmeats? Isn't that what young girls such as yourself always favor—sweetmeats? My own daughters consume a shocking amount of honeyed morsels. Or mayhap your fancy turns to a more savory dish."

Whatever his intent, he had managed to focus the attention of almost every member of the court on the two of them, on her discomfort and his overly solicitous behavior.

"No, please. I'm not hungry."

"But of course you must have hunger," he protested in a voice loud enough to be heard by everyone present. "Why, you have journeyed all the way from—Now let me think, my memory falters. From whence is it you come?"

"I . . ." Sam struggled to come up with a more plausible explanation than the truth.

"Well, you see, I actually came here from . . ."

"Chicken?" He placed a half chicken with feet on the plate and shoved it under her nose. Singed feathers were visible, some only little blackened stumps. She realized that it must have been difficult to remove feathers back then. Someone must have had to pluck them individually. Was there such a profession as a feather plucker? It was a thoroughly revolting thought.

"No, I . . ." For a moment she battled an intense urge to throw up.

"Pie? Lovely pie made of pastry and black-birds. I wager there are more birds in this pie than in any other you have tasted, for the law allows the royal household to pull as many winged creatures from the sky as the king desires. Do they have blackbird pie where you come from?"

From the corner of her eye Sam could see Lady Jane struggling to cross the floor to her. She was being stopped by everyone she passed, each cluster of courtiers grabbing her arm, lips moving swiftly as they quizzed her on Sam.

Jane would never get to her side in time to save her from Northumberland's grilling. Even when she reached her, there would be little enough the petite girl could do to distract him.

It was up to Sam. She had to do something now. Fast.

Then it came to her. The oldest trick in the book. Sam raised her wrist to her forehead, and pretended to faint.

"Ah," she sighed as she crumpled to the ground.

Even as her cheek rested against the rush matting covering the floor, she recognized she had just performed the fakest swoon in history.

"God's wounds," Northumberland spat in annoyance. Obviously he was on to her ploy. "Get up, you little chit."

That didn't matter. Everyone else was distracted, at least for the moment, and she was no longer under Northumberland's laser-sharp inquisition. She had a few seconds to collect herself, to think of a plausible exit line.

There was a great bustle of activity about her, but she was most conscious of the smells on the floor and of the dogs who suddenly began to lick her face and sniff her from head to toe. Then she heard bits of conversation.

"Most peculiar," a woman's voice whispered. "The bodice the strange young lady wears is identical to one missing this very morn from my chamber."

"Are those not Mistress Ellen's sleeves? Yet from two different gowns?"

Sam didn't know whether to cringe, make excuses, or to remain silent on the floor.

"The gable hood is most familiar. Oh, now I do recall where last I saw it. 'Twas upon the old Countess of Salisbury."

"Indeed. Was that before or after her imprisonment in the Tower?"

"Before, most assuredly. And well before her head was struck from her body. Or was that the same one she wore to the block? I cannot recall. What I do remember is that it took a half-dozen blows to remove her head."

At that Sam sat up and yanked off the already wobbly headdress. It had belonged to a dead lady whose head had been chopped off? Maybe even wearing the very same headdress?

"Gross," she exclaimed, and at that she was greeted with a chorus of gasps from the mostly female crowd who had encircled her. Lady Jane was nowhere in sight. She may have been close by, but her diminutive stature kept her hidden for the moment.

Glancing up, all Sam could see was a crowd of unfamiliar women with shocked expressions on their faces. Not a single friendly, or even less-than-hostile, look among the group. She felt like the most unwelcome guest at a party.

Then someone was behind her, hands on her shoulders. Her first thought was that it was Northumberland, but before she could turn around, the entire crowd of women had sunk to their knees.

Was everyone copying her? Sam was confused, not sure where to look and what to do, or why the entire court was facedown on the ground.

Then there was a familiar voice, so close it ruffled her hair.

"Let me assist," he said simply. And with that Edward VI, the king of England, Ireland, and France, lifted Sam to her feet and handed her the headdress.

"Oh, th-thank you," she stammered, turning toward him. What she saw amazed her.

The sickly young man she had met the night before was changed. Gone were the red-rimmed eyes, the unnaturally ashen complexion, the hacking cough. Now he seemed, if not exactly robust, at least well rested. His eyes, dark brown and so sad before, had an unmistakable sparkle now.

"Edward, you look great." Sam smiled. He returned her smile and was about to speak.

Northumberland was the first to rise from

his deep bow. "Your Highness, we rejoice at your most fortuitous return to health. Please God, you will remain in such a vigorous state for many years." He seemed to be addressing the entire court, not just the king. With a theatrical flourish he again bowed as if in acknowledgment of his own powers of elocution.

Describing Edward as vigorous was a bit much, Sam thought, taking in his still-pale skin. Edward turned briefly to Northumberland, then to the rest of the court. "We require privacy, my lords and ladies."

Northumberland again rose. "The king requests you all to leave."

Sam was amazed at how quickly the masses of people could evacuate the room, like a well-executed fire drill, done backward in velvet and fur.

"My Lady Jane," Edward called. "Please remain behind, cousin."

Jane's head remained bowed, and she curtsied three times before approaching King Edward. Once before him, she again sank into a low curtsy and kissed his hand. Belatedly Sam also curtsied a few times and kissed his outstretched hand.

Weird. In all of her times greeting a guy she

knew, never once had she curtsied, much less kissed his hand. Things had become so bizarre by now that, she was beginning to feel slaphappy, beyond caring.

Within moments of the king's asking the room to be cleared, the place was empty except for the four of them and long tables of food and drink. Even the dogs had vanished.

"Wouldn't it have been easier for us to leave and everyone else to stay?" Sam asked.

"Your Majesty," began Northumberland. "I wish to discuss matters of vital importance. Indeed, I was presently going to your chambers for such a purpose."

"Leave us, Northumberland."

Had Edward tossed cold water in the duke's face, he couldn't have been more astonished. "Your Highness?"

"We wish to be alone."

"I . . . but . . ." Northumberland was at a loss for words, clearly an unaccustomed position.

"Good morning," Edward said with an equal combination of formality and finality. Then he turned to Lady Jane.

"Jane, I am most pleased at the attire you found for our guest."

Sam glanced at Northumberland as he backed from the room. Even with his head lowered, pure anger flashed from his eyes. And that fury was aimed straight at one person and one person only.

That person was Sam.

A shiver ran down her back as if an icy finger had traced her spine. Without knowing the precise details, she realized two things: One, the duke was feeling threatened, clearly an experience he resented. Two, wrongly or rightly, he blamed Sam for his present predicament.

Jane had warned her about Northumberland, but Sam hadn't taken the warning seriously. She had assumed that she would wake up at any moment. The charm from her mother still dangled from her neck, and somehow she assumed that link with her normal teenage past would carry her home at any moment.

That wasn't happening, and now she was in a strange time, with a powerful enemy.

"Sam. Angel Sam!"

King Edward was calling her name. Blinking, she turned toward him, still shaken by the lingering image of Northumberland's anger.

"I did as you told and banished the hounds from my chamber as I did slumber. I have not enjoyed such a night since, well, I cannot even recall."

"True, Cousin Edward, you seem even more restored than you did this morning at chapel."

"After chapel I did as Sam told me, Jane. No wheat, which was all I could recall of what I was told. So thus my meal was naught but some partridge, venison, and a little slice of capon. After my fast was broken, there was no sluggish humor within, no coughing. I have not coughed ere last evening!"

The two cousins spoke quickly, as close friends do, their heads together, barely cognizant of the world around them, or of the fact that Sam was perilously close to tears.

She didn't want to be there. All she wanted was to go home, to face the wrath of her dad over the BMW, to fail her history test, and to discover that Kevin the Hunk was dating Stacey the Cheerleader. Even the thought of Jason's stealing the television remote during her favorite music video made her want to sob with longing.

All she wanted was to be home, where she was known, where her every action and word did not require an elaborate explanation. She envied Edward and Jane for their friendship and intimacy. Whatever pressures they encountered, at least they knew who they were, where they fit in the intricate scheme of their world.

She would give anything—a king's ransom—to face her normal torments. Anything.

Again the king was speaking. "So, what say you, Angel Sam?"

She was expected to say something. It didn't really matter what she said. After all, any small element of control she had had over her life was long gone. Probably forever.

"Sure. That sounds great. Whatever."

"Very well," Edward said with authority. "We will begin a royal progress to show our most loyal subjects that they need not fear our health, that we are restored. Lady Jane and Angel Sam shall accompany us."

"Your Highness," Jane said gently. "Perhaps Angel Sam should be called by another name, for the use of 'Angel' may strike fear in some and disbelief in others."

"Yea, in truth you are correct. We do not wish to evoke any ill humor with the court or other citizens. Very well. From henceforth you will be known as Lady Sam of . . ."

"Of the Americas, Your Highness?" Jane offered. "That way you will be staking your claim to the New World, as well as giving Sam a title."

"Excellent!" Then he paused, a keen intelligence evident on his features. He'd probably make honor roll at about any high school back home, Sam mused as Edward tapped his silk-slippered foot. "But think you not the ambassadors of Spain would be alarmed at the title? They are yet concerned with our embracing the true religion over that of Rome. It is a delicate matter, Lady Jane. Mayhap Sam should be granted another title, less likely to offend."

"But we *have* embraced the true religion." An emphatic fire burned in tiny Lady Jane, taking Sam aback with its potency. "And the New World shall be ours. Proclaim her as Lady Sam of the Americas. Announce to the world that you intend to be a real king, not the puppet of Northumberland!"

Edward straightened. "Aye, cousin. This is the dawning of a new era—my era. Thus, I pronounce you Lady Sam of the Americas. But you are still my angel, my talisman of good fortune. Hence you will be with me always, as God wills."

Sam curtsied, as she assumed she was expected to, and listened as they planned her next few weeks. For Lady Sam of the Americas was to join the Tudor clan on a family vacation, the so-called royal progress.

Chapter 6

The stronger Edward became, the more physically well and emotionally confident he grew. After being ill for so many months, his newly restored health filled him with spectacular delight. Now the whole world was open to him. All the pleasures and privileges of his kingdom were there for his enjoyment!

At first his every sense was heightened. The sun seemed more glorious, the grass a deeper shade of green. The air was more fragrant and every bite of food, from a crisp apple to a slice of succulent beef, made his eyes water with pure relish. Women in the court were more enticing than before, jokes were more humorous. Edward, who had been preparing for certain death, was suddenly celebrating life.

Not just any life, but a royal life. The life of a mighty king. He could now revel in all of the excesses of his father, savor the fruits given to him by the great King Henry. This was Edward's privilege. It was as if he had been granted a divine second chance, a rebirth.

Soon, he wanted more. Demanded more. A larger palace at Nonesuch. Perhaps more spacious gardens at Windsor. He began to complain to Northumberland. Was he not the king? Was it not his prerogative to have the best of everything, whenever he desired?

And every bit of Edward's recovery and new set of demands added to Northumberland's resentment of Sam.

The transformation of the king had been astonishing to all who witnessed it. At first some thought him slightly mad, assuming his newly formed eccentricities had been the result of illness combined with royal whimsy. There was great confusion when he banished dogs from the court. For as long as anyone could remember, the sight (and scent) of hounds sniffing at banquets and lounging by the throne had been an accustomed one, even expected. To have them suddenly prohibited was perplexing, to say the least. Many were fond of the dogs, indeed the king's own spaniels were now housed behind the stables at Nonesuch.

It was Northumberland who was forced to

explain to faithful servants of the king that their dogs were no longer welcome.

Then the king issued a decree forbidding the wearing of fur at court. As he did with the banishing of dogs, he gave no further explanation of why furs were no longer permitted. He didn't want the members of his own court to perceive him as physically weak or compromised in any way. Thus no dogs, no furs, and no explanation given. It was a royal command, and that, Edward believed, should be enough.

After all, his word was the absolute law. It was considered high treason to even question the king. To go against his wishes was unthinkable, a mortal sin.

But the British citizens were perplexed. Why was the young king acting with such haste? And with such unbending severity? Some wondered if there might be a reason for this strange behavior. There could be something wrong at court—maybe even a crisis brewing. Could the king's sudden decrees be signals that more confusion was yet to come?

Several years earlier, in a small village in Cornwall, a group of men—terrified by the change of power from Henry VIII to his young son Edward—proclaimed that they would live as they had under Henry's rule. They would follow the old laws as if the late king still lived, as if time stopped before the old king died. Not until the new, untried king reached the age of twenty-four would they follow his commands.

The men were sentenced to death, although only one was actually put to death. It had been a warning to the rest of the kingdom that the new king's word was law, and anyone who went against him would suffer the fate of a traitor.

Now, without explanation, dogs and furs were banished.

Not only were nobles at a loss with what to do with their new and expensive sable cloaks and mink collars, the furriers in London were enraged. How could they survive when their wares were no longer in demand? Who would buy their pelts now? Edward promptly assigned Northumberland the task of finding a resolution.

But that was nothing compared to the outcry of the dairy producers when Edward instructed his cooks to cease using milk, cheese, and butter. Or when farmers learned their wheat would no longer be required in the making of bread for the royal households.

Again, it was Northumberland who was

told to quell the uprisings, to stop trouble before it became a revolution. For the consequences of the king's decrees left open the very real possibility of starvation. Most of the population could only afford bread and cheese; meat was usually reserved for special occasions. Should those foods be banished entirely—and with King Edward's sudden decrees, that seemed a possibility—most of the nation would indeed starve. Faced with even the remote chance of widespread hunger, some citizens began to panic.

None of this had happened until the Lady Sam of the Americas came to court. Edward had been ill and growing weaker by the day, both physically and mentally. He had given up, and Northumberland had taken the reins of power with competent authority. It had been a seamless transition, elegant in its simplicity. Until Lady Sam arrived, Edward had been humbly preparing for a pious, gentle death, leaving Northumberland with the daunting, yet not unrewarding task of running the country.

As the Lord Protector of the Realm—a position he had fought for bitterly, and even committed murder to secure—Northumberland was still the most powerful man in England.

But he saw his grip slipping as Edward flourished. Even Northumberland's considerable powers of charm were wearing thin under the strain of his anger, under the tense negotiations with citizens justifiably outraged by the strange and sudden turn of events.

Change was the one thing most feared by the people. And sudden, unexplained change was nothing short of terrifying. There were no newspapers to analyze events calmly, no reassurances to ease mounting anxiety. The vast majority of the population could not even scratch their given names, much less read documents. Any information given to the general public was usually done so on a local level, by parish priests or village elders. Slow change was accepted, rapid change was not. Even clothing styles remained virtually the same decade after decade, generation after generation.

Northumberland knew this, saw the panic on the faces of the people he now met in the streets and countryside. Their fear was more potent simply because it was unexplained change. It was similar to witnessing a solar eclipse, a natural event the common folk could not understand.

There had been violent uprisings caused by far less than the king's new commands. Just a few years before, in 1549, a series of simple events had almost led to revolution. It had started with the distribution of the new prayer book, which was seen as radical. Very little had been changed, but the language had been brought up to date and the priests were instructed to use less Latin and more English in their services.

The general discontent and fear of the new instructions spilled over into all areas, flamed by those who felt they had much to gain from such violent change. A rebellion was contained, but barely. But Northumberland knew it would take only a single spark to fan the old fears into a terrifying, all-consuming inferno now.

"This was not to have happened," he growled to his wife, the duchess, on one of the increasingly rare occasions when he was at their Syon House estate.

His wife, the former Jane Guildford, did not glance up from her needlepoint. She could ply a skillful needle, as could most well-bred ladies of her time, and she was a gifted social climber. Her weapon of choice was her tongue, which she employed with frequency on her children and husband.

"But it *has* happened, John," she said softly,

stabbing at the butterfly design on the screen. The insect got it right between the eyes. "You have allowed a mere child to usurp your position at court."

"But that child happens to be the king, my dear."

"I do not speak of the king, fool. I speak of that ridiculous Lady Sam. Why, even the name is absurd."

"She is nothing."

"Nay. She is everything. The sickly boy is no longer sickly. He relies on her. She now dictates the royal menu, the royal clothing. He plays at sports, a game she has introduced called 'soccer.' It is said he is fit and healthy, and rivals his late father in athletic prowess."

"We have seen such rallies before in our frail king. Alas, those healthful respites are woefully all too brief."

"It is said the king wishes to marry her."

"The king will make a political alliance when he is ready. At present his health is still uncertain. But later, perhaps in a year, we will select a suitable bride. There is a French princess as well as the young queen of Scots. There is still his cousin Lady Jane as a possibility. When the time comes, I will decide. Until then . . ."

"There will be no 'until then.' He will marry the girl, and there is naught you will be able to do about it."

"I am the Lord Protector," he roared.

"You *were* the Lord Protector." Again the needle pierced the butterfly.

"I shall show you who I am. I shall show the world what sort of force is Northumberland."

With that he slammed from the room. On the face of his wife was, at last, a small smile of satisfaction.

The barge floated up the River Thames on its way to Hampton Court.

Sam closed her eyes, her right hand trailing in the chilly water, savoring the gentle warmth of the springtime sun. The weather was much like the April and early May days at home, the tepid glow of the newly emerging season nipped by one of winter's sudden gusts. Soft, warm days were punctuated by cold, damp nights.

The sounds of the other boats in the royal envoy penetrated her gauzy awareness, the rhythmic rowing of the oars, the shouts of citizens on the riverbank cheering their robust, handsome young king.

Most of the people cheered, although a few

cheese makers and furriers stood in sullen silence. The dog handlers, surrounded by their equally subdued hounds, also remained pointedly silent. Sam thought she heard a few of the dogs growl as Edward waved.

Since she arrived, Edward had made an astonishing recovery. He was completely changed from that sick, pale boy she had first met. The day before, at the house of Lord Someone-or-other, she had seen him without his shirt, fencing with one of his sword masters. From the blushes of the other court ladies, and the double takes of the men, she could tell she wasn't the only one who thought he was surprisingly buff.

Something else had changed as well, though. Something from him was missing that had been so evident that first night. Compassion? Maybe that was it. He had been so kind, so gentle when he was ill. Now he seemed to demonstrate a distinct lack of understanding, an inability or unwillingness to listen. Perhaps he had always been bossy. He was, after all, the king.

Still, the stronger he got, the less he seemed to recognize the wants and needs of others. During the progress, spending several days and nights at the homes of his most loyal subjects, giving them little or no warning of his arrival, he had seemed shockingly unconcerned with the discomfort he was causing. One poor lady was forced to play hostess to the king and his new dietary demands while her husband was away, and she was alone with a handful of disorganized servants and a new baby. Another family was clearly in the midst of some sort of dysfunctional crisis—something about the eldest daughter and a gardener. Still they had to entertain the king and his court at their own expense.

Lady Jane had explained the delicate balance, how they must offer the very best they could afford without displaying too much wealth. The worst offense would be to exhibit more abundance than the king himself possessed. The next worst offense would be not to exhibit enough.

Nothing seemed to satisfy the king. While he seemed pleased enough when he first arrived at an estate, he soon found reason to complain. The food was too bland or too spicy, the rooms too large or too small, the drafts too cold or too warm. He demanded instant gratification, immediate attention to his most trivial whims.

Instead of the basic kindness she had first

seen in the king, Sam was beginning to see flashes of temper. He threw a book at Mr. Cheke, his longtime tutor, when the older man gently reminded him to study the new astronomy charts. He demanded the return of his close friend, some guy named Barnaby Fitzpatrick, even though he was in distant France making diplomatic strides in that country's court. The king wanted his friend home, and he wanted him home now.

"He is my best companion," Edward said to Sam. "There is no one here to match Sir Barnaby. Not a single person comes close." The king had made that statement in a voice loud enough to insult most of England.

"But Your Majesty, isn't it quite a long way for him to travel?" Sam asked.

"Barnaby Fitzpatrick is my companion, but also my subject. Others here are dull. I require him at my side at once."

She didn't dare to question him further on the subject. Actually, any subject seemed to anger him, to fire his increasingly volatile temper.

Sam could tell that even Lady Jane was growing wary of her cousin. And he, in turn, was ignoring the sensible, wise council of the learned Jane for some of his new-found companions, young men who found joy in late-night gambling and impromptu sword play.

Jane didn't say much to Sam, or to anyone, about the changes in Edward. She was far too tactful for that, and far too aware of the court dangers. Instead she turned away whenever court whisperings became too pronounced. She sought comfort in her books, in learning Hebrew—Lady Jane's new passion. Unlike Sam, she simply accepted his new attitude as a king's prerogative.

Things had changed.

Once Sam had tried to discuss the situation with Edward, thinking that perhaps he was not aware that his strict dietary zeal had not been welcome by most of his subjects.

"Your Majesty," Sam said to him as gently as possible. "You do not need to banish all furs from court, or cheese or wheat. Other people seem upset by the changes. Maybe you should just not eat those things, just not wear the furs yourself. That works well for my brother, and . . ."

"But I am the king," he had stated simply. "My needs and desires are the needs and desires of my people."

"Yes, but maybe other people would like a choice and . . ."

"I am king." Then he had left Sam alone so

he could practice archery with some of his men.

She wasn't just thinking of the other people when she had spoken to the king. Frankly, the dwindling choices at mealtime had been bothering her. A cheese sandwich would have been welcome amid the hoofed and footed meats. But whatever the king did, it seemed his people must do as well.

More people applauded as the barge continued down the river, although Sam suspected they had been paid to do so by the harried-looking servants she recognized running on the riverbank just ahead of the envoy. Even then their applause was thin and the cheers more mechanical than genuine.

Didn't he see what was happening? Didn't he realize that if these people were beginning to show resentment, the rest of the country must be feeling much the same way?

She had heard rumblings of discontent. Isolated as she was in the royal household, occasional comments drifted her way. Edward was becoming a remote figure to his people. Unpredictable. Frightening.

This was an age of superstition, when witchcraft and ghosts were accepted facts of life.

Sam took a deep breath. She was beginning to have a terrible sense of foreboding, a feeling of dread. Nothing seemed to feel right. Although she tried to push away the fear, she, too, was every bit as frightened as the citizens of England.

The king stood under a glittering canopy of purple shot with gold. He was almost glowing with health and pure happiness with himself and his world. She opened her eyes slightly to see his figure traced golden in the late afternoon sun. The jewels studding his clothing, the rings stacked on his fingers and the heavy gold chains around his neck sparkled as if in total agreement with the overall fabulousness of the wearer.

"You will enjoy Hampton Court," Edward announced. "My father took possession of it from Cardinal Wolsey. It is rich beyond our other palaces, even Nonesuch. You will find it a relief from the more common dwellings we have suffered during this progress. Tonight we shall have a banquet at Hampton, with musicians and dance."

Sam pretended to be asleep, well aware that she alone was allowed such a liberty as to fake sleep in front of the king. For all of his changes, he still forgave her social lapses. Others were stunned by her boldness, by her lack of ceremony with Edward.

In simple fact she was still uncertain of the social intricacies that were required. While Lady Jane had indeed kept her promise and instructed Sam on the basics of daily life at court, there was still much she didn't understand. She knew how to curtsy and to whom, but wasn't certain about what to call people. Titles such as "sir" to "Your Grace" and everything in between seemed to run together.

Other necessities were just plain omitted by Lady Jane, simply because she had no idea Sam wouldn't know them already. How could she have known that people carried their own dinner knives with them wherever they went? That no one had a fork? That bread was used to scoop up food at even the most formal occasions, and that without bread, spoons and fingers?

Above all, that no one wore underwear.

All of those elegant, stiff ladies in paintings, all of those men looking gallant, the kings and queens and dukes and duchesses . . . and not a single pair of underwear among them. No boxer shorts, no long johns, nothing. Lady Jane had revealed that shocker to her early on, when Sam had asked about getting a new pair of panties.

Edward was laughing at something, or, more probably, someone.

Sam was also aware that her very survival depended upon his dependence upon her. As long as he felt she was vital to his life, she would be protected by him. But the stronger he became, the less he seemed to need anyone, including Sam.

Already she had seen a difference in his treatment of her, subtle, yet noticeable. His expression was no longer eager, waiting for her approval. Now he seldom even glanced at her. Instead he was too occupied with his own whims and pleasures. She was simply a new audience for him.

He had sent for his friend Barnaby Fitzpatrick because he was growing bored, restless. The king wished to be amused, and Sam was no longer amusing enough.

Not that she could blame him. The poor guy had been sick for so long that he deserved to have some fun.

The only question was, at what—or whose—expense would that fun be had?

"Northumberland should be arriving from London presently," Edward said and sighed.

Sam hadn't seen much of the duke since the royal progress commenced. He had been busy with official business, it was said. And Sam, for one, sure hadn't missed him.

"Ah! Behold, Lady Sam. Here is Hampton Court."

Sam opened her eyes fully and raised herself up on her elbow, the purple fringed pillows piled high beneath her. As she shifted her position, the silver necklace and charm her mother had given her glinted. It was a constant reminder of where she had come from, of where she hoped to return.

For now she was in England, on the royal barge, wearing a new red velvet and gold brocade gown—all of the same color and style this time. And in the distance was the splendid Hampton Court.

It was beautiful, she admitted to herself as they approached the orangish yellow palace. Absolutely spectacular. But she had seen so many spectacular, beautiful things lately, she was numb. Lovely houses, pretty things all around, gold and pearls and gems of all colors and . . .

"Methinks this house will pleasure ye," Edward said. "Within walls of splendor are riches of all description. Often come we here."

And people who speak in reverse.

"Nice," she said, in yet another understatement as the barge pulled up to a lavish, ornate dock, the oars pulled straight up like soldiers at attention. Already groomsmen in the Tudor colors of white and green were lined up to assist them off the boat.

As she stepped on to the dock, barely noticing the bowing servants or the ladies bearing silver trays with goblets and drinks and honeyed figs, she felt like crying. How she longed to go home! She'd give anything to go to the mall with friends, to watch a movie on cable TV, even to have Jason listen in on one of her phone calls.

She was tired. Sick of living in such a strange world, of rising before six every morning to sit in chapel and hear prayers in Latin, of going to bed at nine at night because no matter how many candles burned in a room, it never seemed to get bright enough to do anything once the sun went down.

Not that there was anything to do. Most of the books were in Latin or Greek. She was terrible at needlepoint. She didn't know how to do the intricate dances they practiced at night. And the longer she stayed, the less she seemed to have in common with everyone else.

She was a freak.

"Lady Sam—behold the bowling court! And the tilting yard! And . . ."

"Forgive me, Your Majesty, but I am most fatigued from the journey," Sam said. It was true, but even as she said it she saw him stiffen.

"Very well then. Rest at the present. We shall see you at this evening's festivities." Then he turned his back and began talking with a group of young men. He'd throw his head back and laugh loudly and, she thought, rather unpleasantly. The young men would do the same, if a little forced.

She swallowed as she was led to her chamber. This was going to be a very long night.

Chapter 7

After a nap Sam was feeling better, although not absolutely terrific. She still awoke with a jolt when she realized that she was still there, that it had not been a dream. She had been there two weeks now, and was beginning to get used to this time and place. The simple fact that she was growing accustomed to Tudor England made going home seem ever more distant, her own life seem ever more remote and out of her reach.

She was getting used to things, accepting bits of centuries-old everyday life that had seemed wildly unfamiliar when she had first arrived. Now she didn't think twice before plunging her face into ice-cold, brackish water every morning to wash her face. The major production of simply getting dressed was becoming second nature. She was especially pleased when Jane found her a French hood, one of the prettier headdresses. Sam was even becoming something of a dress expert, recognizing a well-cut gown from a lesser one, deciding who would look better in a high, square neckline versus who could get away with a daringly low-cut bodice.

What had been maddening to Sam when she first arrived had now become mere irritations. Clothing itched, shoes pinched—plus there was no right or left shoe, they were both exactly the same. Floppy hose were tied with ribbons, and those floppy hose covered legs that hadn't been shaved in weeks.

There was no such thing as deodorant, and very few people used perfumes. When fragrances were used, they merely mingled and clashed with the other bodily odors. Freshening one's breath meant chewing a few cloves.

No matter what happened, she doubted that her hair would ever be clean again. The smelly, animal fat-based soaps seemed to encourage filth, no matter how many perfumed oils she slathered on afterward. It was as if her entire body were covered with a thin film of pure yuck.

She had almost forgotten what a hamburger tasted like, or a french fry. On the other hand, she had gotten used to turnips and fruit puddings boiled in cloth. The meats no longer grossed her out, the bits of hide on the ham or even rabbit and quail tasted pretty decent.

Another nice aspect was that she was beginning to tell the people apart. At first they all looked like a bunch of velvet-clad, rather short extras in some historical play. Now she saw the members of the court as individuals. Some were kind, others were to be avoided. Soon she recognized who had a sense of humor, who was known to be grumpy, who was the most accomplished gossip. Just as in her time, everyone was different, everyone had his or her own story and set of problems.

There were even a few cute guys, once she got past the tights and swords. One of the families they stayed with on the royal progress had five sons, all Sam's age or a bit older, all funny, smart, and able to play instruments. For long stretches she could lose herself in a moment, enjoy music or a conversation or a beautifully kept garden.

Then it would come back to her with sudden force, that she was far from home. That perhaps she would never again see her family or friends. That no matter how comfortable she felt at times, she was still an outsider.

Would she ever again go to a movie? Or grab a slice of pizza at the mall? It seemed impossible that a few weeks earlier, her bad perm had been the end of the world.

Now she would gladly accept a lifetime of bad perms for the chance to go home.

For the time being she was living day by day, moment by moment. Not that her situation was all that terrible, especially when she considered the alternatives. She had seen enough of sixteenth-century life to realize how fortunate she was to have landed at the feet of a friendly king rather than someplace else in this world of squalor. Thus far, her glimpses into the lives of commoners, even of the lesser nobility, had proved eye-opening, if not downright horrifying.

There had been the vagabonds by the roadside, some hideously disfigured, missing ears and hands as a result of prior offenses and punishments. Beggars of all sorts wandered aimlessly, some with the letter *B* cut into their faces to brand them. There were stockades set up on market days, where the poor unfortunates accused of petty crimes were forced to remain and be the target of rotten fruit and stones. Sometimes they were forced to remain there for days, the subject of abuse, all because they had crossed a neighbor or slighted a person of authority. Some died of hunger, others died of heat in the summer or cold in the winter.

Even the luckier ones had to struggle to survive each day. Common laborers were weighted down with heavy yokes in order to plow their fields. For most, horses were far too valuable to misuse so harshly—better to use people. They toiled from dawn until past dusk for sustenance and shelter. Childhood usually meant working beside the adults, while old age meant hoping for charity.

In the towns it was no better, sometimes worse. Those with a trade worked equally long hours in cramped, darkened rooms. There were strict laws to govern almost every aspect of commerce, from the wool content of a doublet to the amount of impurities allowed in flour. The streets were filthy with horse and livestock waste, as well as the waste tossed into the streets from households and taverns.

Adding to the misery was the constant stench of the tanners, of the butchers. And on every street corner were the beggars, as reviled in town as they were in the country. They were so despised because the fate of a beggar could so easily befall anyone. The most successful merchant was unable to avoid the specter of the ragged vagabond, unable to forget for even one day that a few business reversals or a plunging market could lead him to the streets.

Should you wish to leave town, to escape the suffering, you had best be careful. Criminals lurked on the highways and side roads, as willing to cut your throat as take your purse or shoes.

Life was cheap, except for the privileged few. For the wealthy, life was merely precarious. No one was safe from disease and early death. The Black Death was still spreading fear throughout Europe. Two of Edward's teenage cousins had recently died of a disease called the Sweat. It was said that a victim could be healthy at breakfast and dead by supper.

When someone sneezed, they said "God bless you" just as they did in Sam's time and place. But instead of being an automatic pleasantry, the phrase was uttered in hushed tones, with genuine fear. Did a simple sneeze mean a more fearful sickness was coming? Would the person who sneezed soon be dead?

Sam overheard one lady at court mention that her sister's infant had just died. Sam was about to say how sorry she was, when the lady added, "'Tis no one's fault but her own that she suffers such grief. One should never grow fond of a child until it is well past five years, and even then excessive fondness is always dangerous. Why, where would I be had I devoted myself to the babes, and all three dead in less than a twelvemonth?"

In the vast world of hardship and suffering, of danger and sudden death, Sam knew very well she was more than fortunate to be in the royal household.

Plus there were some pleasures to be enjoyed. Her room at Hampton Court was sumptuous, larger than the one she shared with Lady Jane at Nonesuch, with a lovely view of a courtyard and within hearing distance of a chiming clock. Jane's room was just down the hall, although from what Sam could tell, she had spent most of the day with her tutor. It amazed Sam that Jane could actually prefer hanging out with her teacher, just as Jane seemed amazed that Sam didn't jump at the chance to learn Hebrew.

"But learning is an honor," Jane had said with such enthusiasm that she sounded like some sort of education groupie.

In the meantime the silent court maids

who lurked everywhere had moved Sam's increasingly abundant possessions into her room before she even arrived. The king had given her an ornate walnut bed that could be taken apart and moved, as well as lavishly embroidered silk coverings and a rich satin tester. Every place they stayed on their progress, the appearance of her rooms remained remarkably consistent. A marble-topped table held her new toiletries, also gifts from the king, including a porcelain and silver pot containing a floral perfumed balm and several brushes and combs.

Other courtiers, hoping to gain favor with Edward, offered conspicuous gifts to Sam. Of course the gifts were always presented before an audience, otherwise the display would be pointless. For her one apparent talent of being friends with the king, she now had two swan's feather fans, a peacock feather headdress, and several pairs of silk stockings. Floppy silk stockings.

At least she could more or less understand those things. Other gifts were a bit more ambiguous, such as a creepy little purse embroidered with human eyes, ears and lips, a weirdly shaped metal hook with which to braid her hair, and a set of lumpy pads that were to be slipped under her hair to give it the appearance of being wavy.

The most important gift she had been given was a gold and ruby ring from the king. Although Sam didn't realize the meaning of the gesture at first, Lady Jane had told her it was of the most vital significance.

"Should you ever be in peril of any sort, send this to the king at once, and he will immediately come to your aid," Jane had explained. Meantime Sam wore it on her thumb, the only place it would fit, even though she thought it was clunky and just a little bit tacky.

Grabbing an apple from a side table just outside her room, Sam decided to explore Hampton Court. It was indeed lavish and lovely, but less self-consciously so than Nonesuch, which seemed to exist merely to impress. Hampton actually had an element of warmth to it, a feeling of comfort. At least it was comfortable considering there was no running water, flushing toilets, electricity, or window screens.

The grounds were even more pleasant than the interior, at least to Sam's way of thinking. The gardens were neat without being overly planned, the new flowers of spring just beginning to burst forth with glorious colors. There were well-trimmed shrubs fashioned in the shapes of exotic animals. Topiary hedges, someone had told her they were called. A winding path of pink gravel led her to a marble fountain, and at frequent intervals along the path there were stone benches with curved legs and curlicue designs.

She could almost forget her situation, if only an airplane would fly overhead, or if she could hear the sound of a boom box playing hip-hop music. It was the silence that bothered her most about this time, now that she was becoming used to the pungent smells and strange sights.

Then suddenly she heard something familiar. It was a girl's voice humming a tune. Although it wasn't quite off-key, it wasn't quite on-key either. It was a lively tune, the pure sound of someone who enjoyed music. It could have been Sam herself trying to replicate her favorite new song from an MTV video or the radio.

Sam followed the sound, and through a clearing in the hedges she saw a girl with very long strawberry blond hair. Her dress was plain, with no adornment whatsoever to lessen the severity of the gray velvet and white cuffs and collar.

In spite of her prim dress, there was something vibrant about the girl. Her hair was free of any headdress or even ribbons, swinging in the afternoon sun. Her presence seemed to dapple the whole garden with infectious energy. She was alone, but enjoying herself, humming and dancing with an imaginary partner.

Then she stopped, as if the partner held her hand and perhaps kissed it. She smiled coyly. Then she turned and curtsied deeply. Speaking softly to the pretend partner, she blushed and tilted her head at the imaginary eloquence of the suitor.

Sam watched in fascination and a little jealousy as the girl laughed, clearly delighted with whatever Mr. Invisible had just said. How wonderful to glean such happiness from the air!

"Oh, how I wish," Sam said to herself. If only she could have such an imagination, perhaps then she could be happy again, at least at times.

All at once the girl stiffened and whirled in one neat motion.

"Declare yourself at once," she proclaimed in a tone that was anything but girlish.

"Hello," Sam said tentatively, stepping

forward from the bushes. "I'm sorry. I didn't mean to spy."

"How dare you." Although she seemed only a few years older than Sam, if that, she was in absolute command of the situation. Her back straightened, and even though she was about the same height as Sam, she suddenly seemed to tower over her. The only indication of her previous girlish persona was a single sprig of flowers still entwined in her glorious waist-length mane.

"I'm so sorry," she stammered. "I . . . well. Can you show me how to do that?"

"I repeat, declare yourself at once."

"Oh, yes. Sorry. I'm Sam McKenna. I don't mean to intrude, but . . ."

"You are Lady Sam." The young woman scanned her from head to toe. The results of her evaluation, whether favorable or not, were impossible to determine, for her expression did not change. Her eyes were an intense shade of golden brown, almost tawny, and seemed to sparkle with intelligence. "I have heard much of you."

"Thank you. I think. And who are you?"

"Well, that depends." Her voice had a surprisingly rich timbre for such a young woman. "Some call me the Lady Elizabeth. Others call me Princess Elizabeth. On occasion I am called the illegitimate daughter of the late king. But rarely am I called that to my face."

Sam was stunned. This was Queen Elizabeth! Even she knew the importance this young woman would play in history.

"Oh my God!" Sam sank into her deepest curtsy. And this time she really meant it. "You're Queen Elizabeth! Oh my God . . ."

"Hush," she whispered, not without a hint of humor in her tone. "Unless you wish to be accused of treason."

Sam looked up and shook her head in confusion.

"Great heavens, you are a dolt. Rise at once," Elizabeth said in exasperation. Sam did as she was told. Then Elizabeth lowered her voice. "Do you not know that calling me 'Queen' infers the death of the present monarch and is thus considered treason?"

"I . . . No. I did not." Sam could not help but stare at her. After all, she would be the most famous queen in British history, one of the most glorious figures in any history for that matter. And there she was, just inches away, a crumpled daisy hanging in her hair.

And like Lady Jane, she had freckles. Sam smiled.

"What? The notion of treason amuses you?"

"No, no. I just . . ." Sam thought for a moment. Here she was, face-to-face with the most incredible mind of the Tudor age. So she asked her the most logical of questions. "Could you teach me how to dance?"

"What mean you?"

"I don't know how to dance here."

Elizabeth raised her palms in confusion and arched her thinly drawn eyebrows, and Sam clarified. "I have been here for some weeks, Princess Elizabeth. I have been under the most kind tutelage of Lady Jane. As wonderful as she has been, I have not had a chance to . . . well. We have done a great deal of discussing. I now know of Plato, Socrates, and the basic teachings of Erasmus. Theology is another biggie with her. Jane is great, really. Don't get me wrong. But . . ."

Then Elizabeth smiled. "My cousin Jane is a most wondrous tutor, as you say. But she has a deep aversion to any sort of display. Dancing, I fear, is a most shameless form of display."

"Yes, it is." Sam nodded.

Elizabeth continued. "Jane does not

approve of the more trifling pastimes. I myself, however, feel one must temper scholarly pursuits with those of a more frivolous nature. Perhaps a small display. Tell me, has she not taught you how to dance a single step?"

"No! And I have wanted to, but she thinks it's foolish. I hear the musicians, and a few times I've been asked to dance, but I haven't a clue how to begin. I'm too embarrassed to try in front of all those people at court. It all seems so complicated. But they do seem to be having fun."

"Perhaps I may help you, Lady Sam," she said. "Have you ever heard of the volta?"

Sam shook her head no.

And then, in the garden at Hampton Court, with no other accompaniment than their own humming, the future Queen Elizabeth taught Sam how to dance.

It was to be a celebration of sorts.

King Edward, who had not seen his half sister Elizabeth for almost a year, was to be reunited with his closest sibling. Like Edward, Elizabeth had been schooled in the new progressive way of thought, with enlightened tutors from the Continent. They had similar viewpoints, Edward and Elizabeth. Their father had been the Henry VIII of his later middle years, not the fiery young buck of the first part of his reign. Elizabeth was the product of his second wife, Anne Boleyn, so famously beheaded to make way for the new wife who would hopefully bear the much-longed-for son and heir. Edward was the product of that third marriage, a union also cut short by untimely death.

Mary, his other half sister, was not there at Hampton Court. She was at her own household of Hunsdon in Hertfordshire. Daughter of the first of Henry's six marriages, she had not been invited to the celebration of her brother's restored health. Much older than Edward or Elizabeth, Mary was nearing forty, unmarried, removed to a distant estate, and embittered by years of exile and neglect. She had seen her beloved mother Queen Catherine humiliated, cast aside by her father when he desired another wife. Mary herself had been tossed away and declared illegitimate when her father married a new wife. Even when the new wife was divorced and beheaded, there was no triumph for Mary. The birth of her brother had ensured her ultimate dismissal.

But that didn't matter for now. Mary would not be missed, nor even thought of. Tonight there were to be the finest musicians, the most accomplished dancers, tumblers and jugglers and clowns of every sort. There would be tables laden with food, from massive roasts of beef and pork and mutton to smaller but no less impressive dishes of capons, goose, wildfowl, swan, pheasant and—to Sam's horror—pigeons. Tremendous silver platters were strewn with great salmon, oysters, and so many smaller types of fish they seemed to have drained the entire ocean. There were heaping bowls of peas and turnips, parsnips and carrots, leeks and cabbage and several sorts of beans.

Then there were tarts, savory and sweet, and pastries. The cook had somehow persuaded the king that there was very little flour in such concoctions, for they were decorative, more for display than for consumption.

"People will not eat them," assured the cook. "They will simply stare at the magnificence of their king's majesty!"

The king had believed it. So there were elaborate creations, pies with hunting scenes layered on top and sugared wafers arranged in replicas of the Tower of London and Windsor Castle. It was more art than pastry, with each structure more fantastic and impressive than the last. Boiled puddings were brimming with fruits, and gold pots overflowing with honey dotted every sideboard.

Dozens of silver and gold pitchers held ale, wine, and hypocras, a rare, sweet potion imported all the way from exotic lands. Sam's influence had prompted the addition of fruit juices mixed with boiled water, which the king had eagerly embraced after she promised him that boiling the water would make the notoriously impure English water safer to drink.

The great hall had never looked more magnificent, festooned with floral garlands, yards of gold cloth lavishly draped around columns and beams, even spread upon the floor in the ultimate display of regal abundance. More than one of the courtiers mentioned that it was every bit as lavish as a grand state occasion. To Sam, it looked like a fairy-tale palace.

Now this was one evening she was actually looking forward to, especially since she had been introduced to the basics of court dance. There was a sense of excitement bubbling as evening approached.

Princess Elizabeth and Sam had spent the entire afternoon practicing the various steps, usually with Elizabeth taking the role of the man so she could instruct Sam on how to move properly. Some of the paces reminded her a great deal of the Virginia reel, which she'd learned in junior high gym class.

But the fun part had been dancing with Elizabeth. There was an almost electric quality to her personality, a radiant spark that seemed to make everything glow. Her laughter was infectious, although it wasn't easy to evoke. But when Sam removed her stiff French hood, revealing her parched, frizzy hair, Elizabeth doubled over in giggles.

Apparently some of Sam's dance moves also tickled the future queen's funny bone, although Sam herself couldn't figure out what was so amusing.

"What's wrong with my twirl?" Sam asked. "Didn't I twirl just the way you showed me? I've always been a good twirler."

All Elizabeth could do was shake her head and bite her lip in an obvious attempt to save Sam's feelings.

"Perhaps with a proper partner, you will again regain your twirling prowess."

By the time she was getting dressed for the evening's festivities, Sam felt as if she had a new friend in Elizabeth. There was a strangely modern aspect to Elizabeth's personality, an undeniable, indefinable quality of crisp awareness that made her blend perfectly with her surroundings, yet stand out at the same time. Even her physical features were somehow timeless, with her small waist and impatient, athletic movements. Her face, while not classically beautiful, was unforgettable, with a strong aquiline nose, flashing eyes, and a mouth that seemed to be perpetually on the verge of a smile. No doubt she would be just as clever and hip in Sam's time—or in any other age—as she was in her own.

The musicians were already playing when she first entered the great hall. Guests were milling about, goblets were being filled, the hum of conversation was punctuated by bursts of laughter.

Sam was no longer intimidated by the mere thought of entering a full hall. She did not have to wait for Lady Jane, who was usually late because of her reluctance to rub elbows with the rest of the court.

Now Sam was feeling positively good about herself, her lack of twirling ability aside. Her gown, with deep green sleeves and a brilliantly colored embroidered bodice, was most certainly one of the nicest in the room. Her rounded French hood felt much more natural than the gabled hoods she had worn at first, although this one, too, was borrowed from Lady Jane. Sam thought the gold beaded rim and dainty stitching was lovely. It also covered most of her hair, which was still an absolute mess. On top of the frizzy perm was dirt and soap scum. Without conditioner and proper shampoo, but with only ice-cold basins of water, Sam understood why headdresses would be in fashion for the next few centuries.

Suddenly the musicians played an ornate fanfare, and from behind a velvet curtain emerged Edward, followed by Elizabeth. The king was attired in white and gold, with large drop pearls dangling from the rim of his hat, from his sleeves, and even from the pommel of his sword. A flowing cape of white silk shot with gold covered his padded shoulders. All in all, he looked like a spectacular decoration from a department store Christmas window. He grinned, glowing with health, and motioned for Elizabeth to step beside him.

The princess was also impressive, although far less ostentatious than her brother. Her gown was of a more subdued yellow, which mirrored the king's without eclipsing his impact.

"Good move, Elizabeth," Sam said to herself at her new friend's demure behavior.

There was wild applause, and Sam had the strange sensation of being at a royal pep rally.

When the applause ebbed, the musicians launched into more sedate background music. Sam wasn't quite sure where to go, which cluster of people with whom to mingle. She could now chat easily about jousting, court tennis, and the king's wonderfully improved health. Or, if need be, she could talk about the new fashions from Europe, the pros and cons of the most recent farthingales from France, and about the new taste sensation from the Americas, a root vegetable called a "potato."

"Is it true, Lady Sam, that you have actually eaten a potato?"

"Yes, Lady Anne, I have," Sam replied, once again stumped as to how to describe the taste of a potato. She was no longer riveted or appalled by Lady Anne's dark, and in some spots missing teeth.

The musicians were beginning to play more lively tunes, the sounds of the skin drum, lute, and assorted reed instruments were now familiar to her. Some of the songs were becoming her favorites, and as Lady Anne continued talking, Sam glanced around the hall. A few people were beginning to bounce on their heels and tap their feet, a sure sign that dancing was imminent.

Then she saw him.

He was tall, with hair so dark it was almost black. He stood out not only because of his height and distinctive coloring, both rare before good nutrition and dyed hair, but because of a certain presence. Charisma, Sam thought to herself. That's what he had. Everyone else was dull brown, he was a riot of exploding colors.

It had nothing to do with what he was wearing. Unlike Edward, his clothing was restrained, almost plain. From what she could see in the candlelight and by light of the six-foot fireplace, he wore a simple black doublet, dark hose, with a white unadorned shirt underneath. At his side was a sword, the hilt free of jewels. The metal glinted as he moved. He stood with several other young men, and they all laughed at something he said. He added something else, and they all laughed even harder. It wasn't the forced laughter she had seen with the king and his friends. These guys seemed to take genuine delight in the young man.

Abruptly, as if aware of being watched, he glanced in her direction. He looked right at her, and for a moment she looked over her shoulder to see if he was staring at someone else. But there was no one else around her, and Lady Anne had turned away, refilling her goblet and removing a turret from the biscuit rendition of the Tower of London. Like the other sugar-mad members of the court, Lady Anne was devouring the welcome pastries at an alarming rate.

It felt like a movie. Their eyes met, this mysterious young man's expression changed. The smile left his face, and he very slowly bowed. She wasn't quite sure how to act. No one had ever bowed to her from across a room. So she curtsied, as if they had just been introduced, even though he was still many yards away.

He said something to his friends, and within a few seconds he was at her side.

"Good evening," he said and bowed again. This time he took her hand, and for a moment she thought he would kiss her wrist. But he didn't. He simply held her hand in his, and it felt absolutely wonderful.

Her mouth was dry, and she wondered if any sound would come out if she tried to speak. Up close he was even more gorgeous than he was across the room.

Even in the rather silly hat, like a puffy

beret, he looked terrific. His hair was indeed dark, but with the kind of streaks you get from being out in the sun a great deal. His eyes were a deep green, such a strange, fathomless color, surrounded by impossibly dark lashes. There was a very slight stubble on his chin and across the lean cheeks, and in her mind she wondered how very difficult it must be to shave with a straight razor.

"Hello," Sam said at last. Had the word actually come out?

When he smiled, his teeth were white and even, except for one slightly crooked tooth on the top.

"You are the famous Lady Sam, are you not?" His voice was deep, but his accent was more pronounced than the others, a gentle rolling lilt.

"Well, Sam I am." Why did she always sound like Dr. Seuss when she tried to speak like the rest of them?

But he simply smiled. "I am Sir Barnaby Fitzpatrick."

"Oh, the king has mentioned you!" All she could do was smile at him.

Barnaby. That was one of those names that could go either way, hideous or great, depending on the particular Barnaby in question. In this case, it was definitely great.

She tried to remain cool. "Do you come here often?" The moment the words were out, she wanted to take them back. Of all the stupid things to say . . .

Barnaby didn't act as if she had been stupid. "Aye, Lady Sam. But I did not go on the recent progress, as is my usual custom. Business kept me abroad. I am glad to at last meet the famous Lady Sam. All of the court is speaking of you."

"Oh." She nodded. Okay, she thought to herself. What next. Something pithy and amusing. "I hope they're saying nice things."

Please, she prayed silently. Please, may he not have heard that.

He had heard it. He laughed, then he let go of her hand. "Forgive me," he said, as if holding her hand for too long were some sort of social crime. "I have heard most marvelous things from all, most especially the king."

She swallowed. What was it about his eyes? Yes, he was incredibly good-looking, but there was something else there. Something she recognized, although she couldn't figure out exactly what it was.

"How do you know the king?" It was difficult to keep her thoughts clear with

Barnaby so very close. "He didn't explain how you met. Are your parents connected with the court?"

That question seemed to surprise him slightly. "I am the king's whipping boy."

"Excuse me?"

"Well, not any longer. He knighted me for my pains."

"What on earth is a whipping boy?"

That devastating smile crossed his face. "You are indeed new here, my Lady Sam. When His Majesty first became king upon the death of his father, a curious problem arose."

"It did?"

"Yes. For now he was king, but he was only nine years old at the time. It is an age that can be quite difficult."

Sam thought of her brother Jason, who had just turned ten. "It sure can," she said.

"Occasionally," he continued, then stopped and raised his eyebrows, "perhaps best alter that to 'frequently,' the boy king was in need of punishment. But how to punish a boy before whom the entire court, including his ministers and tutors, even the most high-born lords and ladies, must grovel? Certainly he cannot be touched."

"I never thought of that," she said honestly.

"I don't suppose a time-out would work. So what did they do?"

"They beat me instead."

Sam was unable to hold in her gasp. He quickly spoke. "It wasn't so terrible. In a way I felt sorry for the king. Usually he cried harder than I did at the punishment. He has told me it was far worse on him than it was on me, although he never had to sit down after a session with the whip."

"Why you?" She longed to reach out and touch him.

He shrugged. "I was fortunate."

"How on earth can that be fortunate?"

"Please, lower your voice, Lady Sam. You must understand, I was sent to England as a hostage."

"Oh my God!"

"My father was a powerful Irish chief. I was given to King Henry as a promise of peace, to ensure that my father and our people would not rise up against the English. Since I was but a couple of years older than Edward, and of noble birth, we were schooled together. They knew not what else to do with me, for like you I was alone in this vast place. They couldn't very well let me fend for myself. Nor could they allow me to reside with another noble family, for the tides of favor change too quickly within the court. I was a hostage of England, and thus had become the responsibility of England. Finally someone happened upon the idea of whipping boy, and at last I was put to use. What is wrong, Lady Sam?"

"It's just that . . . well . . ." She felt a sudden pang. "I thought I saw something familiar about you. And now I know what it was. You're lonely, too, aren't you?"

He seemed startled. "I do not think I have ever thought of that."

"I mean, you don't have any family here either. We're both dependent upon the king for our very lives."

"Yea, but in a sense all are dependent upon that," he said quietly, uncomfortably.

Sam looked away. He knew exactly what she felt. Everything seemed to go blurry, and she knew if she stayed a second longer she would start to cry.

"Excuse me," she mumbled. The door to the courtyard was just beyond the next gold-draped column. Blindly she ran, groping along the gold cloth-covered wall until she found the door, and heaved her weight into the massive wooden door to escape.

And in her desire to be alone, she was

totally unaware of the new arrival at the celebration. He had come in late, the dust from his journey still clinging to his cloak, well after Edward's glorious entrance. But he made his way to the sovereign immediately. For he had seen Lady Sam and Sir Barnaby leave the hall in great haste, and knew that it would be of considerable interest to the king. Very considerable indeed.

Chapter 8

Alone. She needed to be alone for just a few moments.

Gravel crunched under her feet in the courtyard, the sounds inside muffled, the strains of a dance tune eerie and vague. The fresh, green scent of newly pruned shrubbery was a welcome relief from the press of overly warm bodies in the hall. Taking a deep breath, a calming sense of momentary relief flowed through her. She could think here, she could try to make sense out of the less than sensible way she was feeling.

When her eyes adjusted to the night, she made her way to a stone bench just across the lawn. Odd thoughts crossed her mind, flashes of memory that had nothing to do with this time. She thought of other parties long ago, of stepping onto freshly cut lawns with stereos blaring in the distance. She thought of all the times she would feel something for a guy, and then spend the next week talking her feelings to death on the phone or during school with all of her best friends, especially Lori.

This was so different. Perhaps her emotions had gone haywire simply because the rest of her life had gone haywire. Maybe if Barnaby Fitzpatrick had sat next to her in study hall instead of emerging with a sword like some kind of paperback novel hero, she could keep her rioting feelings in perspective.

But how could she keep those emotions in perspective when her perspective had been switched?

This wasn't fair. Nothing was fair.

Gratefully she sat down, barely noticing the chill that permeated her layers of petticoats and thick velvet skirt. She just needed to think, to get a grip on herself. This was indeed a strange time, but the one thing that had been made abundantly clear was that it was a dangerous time. She could not allow herself to be herself to anyone. Already she had risked a great deal by revealing too much of herself to the king, to Lady Jane, and, to a lesser extent, Princess Elizabeth. Her luck had held thus far, but she would be foolish to put herself at risk with this new stranger.

Why was she so freaked out by Sir Barnaby Fitzpatrick? Of course he was almost movie-star handsome. And then there was his accent, so wonderful in a place where odd accents were the norm. In this era, before television blended all the quirks and unique bends of a region's way of speaking into one bland style, his accent was more lilting than the others. She wondered if he had spoken Irish Gaelic as a child, for from the brief conversation they had shared, he seemed to select his words carefully.

Or maybe it was because he alone really understood what it was like to be an outsider. He, too, did not belong at court.

"May I sit down?"

Sam jumped when she heard his voice, but somehow she was not surprised. He had followed her out, and now he was standing beside her, not three feet away.

"Okay." She looked up at him, and even in the muted light Sir Barnaby was staggeringly handsome.

He did not sit down, though. Instead he stood, shifting uncertainly.

"Forgive me," he said. "But what mean you by 'okay'?"

"Oh. I forgot. Sure, go ahead. Sit down."

Yet another reminder that even the simplest of communications was impossible for her, as if she needed another reminder. Everything required translation.

The bench was quite small, and when he sat down their legs touched. His sword clanked against the side of the bench, and he held his hand over it to still the motion, a gesture to which he was clearly accustomed.

Sam folded her arms as if suddenly cold, although she really wasn't. It was just such a strange sensation to think that a cute guy roughly her own age would be as used to sitting down with a sword as normal guys back home were used to wielding a baseball bat, or shifting a backpack. Or switching the television remote.

"Are you unwell?" There was concern in his voice.

She shook her head, and he just stared at her. She could feel his gaze, although she looked straight ahead and pretended that she didn't notice he was watching her.

They sat in silence for what seemed to be a very long time, although in reality she knew it was only a few minutes. A single song was played inside, a merry little tune that sounded like a galliard, one of the dances she learned that afternoon. They were not alone in the courtyard very long.

"What think you?" he asked in that backward talk.

The sky was bright and cold and dark, with stars glittering like those on some impossible stage set. Back home the sky was so different because no matter where you went, there were bright lights. Even in the country there were airplanes and distant city lights and small country roads with street lamps and cars with their bright headlights beaming in the night.

This was complete darkness. Nowhere on the earth were there lights as bright as the ones she used to flick on every day. So many things that seemed so ordinary back home were really quite extraordinary after all. Her clothes, her CD player. Even her teachers.

How Lady Jane would love high school history!

Sam smiled, remembering. Something about Barnaby urged her to talk. Maybe he made a gesture, or just the way he was watching her caused her to verbalize what she was thinking.

"I had a history teacher once who said that the only real events in history are the ones that have a ten-year significance." Funny, it was strange to think of Mr. Novack now. "He said that sometimes people in the middle of earth-shattering events don't know it at the time. It's only later, much later, that they can trace all the changes to one single moment where everything altered. To one fatal decision that was made, or maybe to one that wasn't made."

She knew she was rambling. It didn't matter, not really, because he couldn't possibly understand what she was saying.

"I understand," he said.

She almost laughed. "No you don't. There is no way you could get it. But that's okay. I don't expect you to understand."

He spoke as if she hadn't just discouraged him. "My ten-year significance was that I did not obey my parents."

"Excuse me?"

He shrugged. "I was told to stay behind that day. My father was to ride out to meet some British soldiers, maybe an ambassador. I recall not. They told me to stay behind, but I followed my father because I wished to see real soldiers. There was a skirmish. I came forward to find my father. And soon I was a hostage, sent from my home in Ireland to this court in England. I became the whipping boy, the companion and confidant of the prince, the fellow pupil of the king. I learned about affairs of the world, about how power shifts and personalities change the course of wars. Now I am Sir Barnaby Fitzpatrick all because I did not obey my parents. I've never been home since, have not seen my family. Nor am I likely to ever go home."

He kicked a piece of gravel with the toe of his shoe. "That may not have been a great historical moment, but for me it was my defining moment. One of my own ten-year significance."

Then he looked at her, and she smiled. "You're right, you do understand."

"I do. But seldom am I given such an opportunity to show that I understand."

Again they sat in silence, longer this time. She wondered if she should speak, confide that she, too, was there simply because she had not obeyed her parents. But she decided not to. There was no point, not really.

"I admire your charm," he said at last.

In spite of her confusion, she smiled. "I have to confess, no one else has ever called me charming."

"That was not what I meant."

She turned to look at him, surprised for a

moment that his face was so close to hers. Then he laughed, and it was a rich, wonderful sound to her ears. "Nay! Forgive me. Indeed you are charming. But I spoke of your charm, the silver charm about your neck."

Her face heated with a blush, but he didn't seem to notice. "It is most unusual. Silver, is it not?"

"Yes. Um, my mother gave it to me for my last birthday."

"Did she? It is beautiful."

Her hand reached up to touch it, and she felt the curls and the ornate designs. Suddenly he placed his hand over hers, lifting the necklace toward him. His fingers were long. She dropped her hand to her lap while he examined the charm.

His dark brows were drawn in concentration as he rubbed his thumb over the silver. Then, as if jolted, he let go. Taking a deep breath, he closed his eyes.

"Are you all right?" she asked.

At first he didn't respond, and she reached out to touch his shoulder.

"Sir Barnaby?"

His vivid green eyes opened. "I know not what was wrong," he mumbled. "The entire world seemed to spin. Did you feel it as well?"

Their faces were only inches apart, and he blinked once, then his eyes seemed to pierce right through her. Slowly his hand rose, and with exquisite gentleness he touched her cheek.

His hand was calloused and rough. From horses, she thought distractedly. He must ride a lot of horses. And jousting. He's probably an expert jouster. And swordplay. Of course, swords.

Then his hand tilted her head just slightly, his thumb under her chin. And his lips parted before they met hers.

Sam felt as if the breath had been knocked from her body. She'd been kissed before, a few times at parties, or after one of those awkward blind dates. But this was entirely different. This wasn't just a young boy with popcorn on his breath wearing a T-shirt with a heavy metal band logo. Sir Barnaby Fitzpatrick was only a year or so older than she was, yet he was a man, a vital, alive man.

Her eyes closed as she lost herself to her rioting emotions. Somewhere in her mind she noted the prickle of his whiskers, the surprising softness of his lips. He smelled like leather and something else, not quite spicy and not quite sweet but absolutely wonderful.

She reached up and touched his hair, thick and just a little wavy, and her hand slid to his neck. A pulse throbbed there, and suddenly she felt as if she had never before known anyone as well as she knew this young man.

"What a delightful picture," a male voice nearby rasped.

Barnaby pulled away, leaving Sam confused, more than a little disorientated. Only his firm grip on her arm steadied her.

"Your Grace," he said, and Sam looked up to see the Duke of Northumberland standing before them. Barnaby rose to his feet, giving her a courtly assist as she, too, stood unsteadily. Then as he bowed, Sam—recovering her senses—curtsied.

"The king requested I follow his two most favored subjects from the great hall. Your exit was so very swift and conspicuous, His Majesty was concerned for your welfare. Yet I confess, what I have discovered is something of a surprise. A delightful picture, to be sure. I am sure the king will be fascinated by my findings."

Sam looked at Barnaby, who merely smiled casually at the duke. "Your Grace is always most attentive to his duties."

"And you, sir, are always derelict. Have a

care. More valuable men have seen their heads roll. You are not invincible, Fitzpatrick."

"No one is, Your Grace."

The tension was almost palpable, and she noticed that Barnaby had slipped his hand to the hilt of his sword. The duke, even in his plush velvet robes of office, looked as if he would like nothing better than to run Barnaby through with his own jeweled dagger. There was clearly a long history of animosity between the young, dashing knight and the older, power-hungry duke.

"Um, did you have a pleasant journey, Your Grace?" Sam asked, hoping to lighten the mood. "Your presence was missed on the royal progress."

The duke's eyes flashed. "A pleasant journey? You ask if I had a pleasant journey? Yes indeed, Lady Sam. It was a most pleasant excursion. Marvelous indeed. My journey consisted of quieting the various rebellions caused by you, our lovely Lady Sam."

"Caused by me?" She was just returning to her senses, trying to follow his meaning. "But I've just been with the court, with the king and Lady Jane. I have not been out at all!"

"With the king. Aye, that is the trouble," the duke turned his full attention to Sam.

"Where shall I commence? First, there are the furriers of London, who have united in alliance with the bread bakers in violent protest of the king's new diet and wardrobe. The farmers are none too pleased either, as their very best wheat is now to be fed to livestock rather than to be used in breads. The common people have now been denied the one food item upon which they could always depend, bread, of course, so there are widespread rumors of uprisings all over the country. Famine. Do you know what hunger does to a man? Do you know what hunger does to an entire village?"

"I d-do not understand," she stammered. "How could this be happening? All I wanted was to help the king."

"That you did. You have helped him become ruler over a land of discontent. You must recall what happened with the crop failures."

"No," she whispered.

"Northumberland," Barnaby began.

"Let me tell her, Sir Barnaby!" Northumberland continued. "This nation rests on a delicate balance. I have helped to preserve that balance. There is superstition amongst the people, genuine fear. When the crops failed several seasons in a row we were able to avert starvation even as the population rioted. We held tight and the situation passed. The new prayer book caused widespread rebellion, but that, too, was contained. With difficulty, it was contained. You, my dear Lady Sam, have been a disaster of biblical proportions. I have seen it with my own eyes. The people are perplexed, they no longer trust their king. And that, my dear Lady Sam, is how rebellion takes hold and spreads. Look about you. And the face that will stare back will be the face of fear itself."

Sam shook her head in confusion, but the duke didn't seem to notice. "May I continue? Then there are the feral dogs, let loose by their owners to run wild. Hounds are no longer in fashion. But soon they will be—on the tables of the starving folk. Then there is Spain."

"Spain?" Sam and Barnaby both said in unison.

"Indeed. The ambassadors from Spain have informed us that the Spanish king will declare war on England unless we retract our claim on North America. By declaring you Lady Sam of the Americas, the king has all but invited war, which will most likely unfold within a fortnight."

"Your Grace, I had no idea . . ." she began.

"Of course you did not! So part of my most enjoyable journey entailed raising an army to defend this island from invasion, which is not a simple task, for most of the mercenary soldiers in England are, in fact, Spanish. Given a choice, and given the ample funds from Spain, they prefer to fight for their own nation. So they are already on these shores, armed, well fed on British beef and eager to battle us. Have I mentioned the war with France?"

"France?" Sam could barely speak.

"Northumberland, you twist the facts to suit your needs," Barnaby said.

"Perhaps I do at times. But not now. France. Yes indeed. They have joined with Spain in a most unholy alliance. As I speak the French army is gathering strength near Calais. And of course they have been given a comfortable home in Scotland, so they may attack us from more than one border. In a matter of weeks, Lady Sam, you have managed to evoke civil rebellion and war with Spain, France, and Scotland. "

"Why have I heard nothing of this, Your Grace?" Barnaby asked. "Why has the king mentioned nothing of these calamities to me?"

"Because the king is distracted! Because

the king will no longer heed his ministers, unless it concerns some form of enjoyment. He cares not what is happening beyond his immediate sight. But he will care, mark my words. I will make him care."

Even as he spoke, the duke's pale complexion became florid, his voice rose, his hands clenched. The great golden chains about his neck clanked together. "Because his restored health could not have come at a worse time. Before you came, he was a thoughtful youth, reflecting on his everlasting soul, preparing to leave his kingdom in the most capable of hands. But he has suddenly been given a gift of vitality, and now he thinks of nothing but sampling the pleasures of this life. Woe be to us should this sudden and remarkable recovery be permanent. We shall all suffer."

"Do you begrudge our sovereign his very life?" Barnaby asked mildly, although Sam knew his words were meant to provoke. "Or is your fury sparked because those most capable of hands waiting to receive the kingdom happen to be your own hands?"

"Do not dare to twist my words, boy," he spat, stepping forward.

"Please." Sam felt ill. "Please stop." Then she turned to Barnaby. "All I wanted to do was help," she said softly. "I did not understand. I had no idea. This is just like with the car, with my father's BMW. I did not mean to hurt anyone. He was sick, the king." Rubbing her temples, which had started to throb, she glanced back at the duke. "This is a celebration after all. Maybe we should just—" Sam began, but the duke cut her off.

"Speak not to me. You have chosen unwisely, my lady. You had a choice with whom to ally yourself, and you selected Lady Jane. I am told you passed the afternoon with the Lady Elizabeth. And now you are with him." The duke's long finger pointed accusingly at Barnaby. "Most unwise. All three will soon fall, and they will pull you down with them."

"Does Your Grace threaten Lady Sam?" Barnaby spoke so softly, she could barely hear the words. His meaning was clear by the edge to his tone, though.

Sam looked between the two men, and suddenly realized the situation could easily get even more out of hand. She had to do something. Now.

"Sir Barnaby," she said in a falsely cheerful voice, pulling his hand from his sword and tucking her arm through his. She tried to ignore the sickening feeling that was beginning to overtake her. She hoped that court manners could somehow keep them from battling each other. At least for the time being. "Please, I would love to dance."

For a long moment the two men remained motionless, as if she did not exist. They just glared at each other like two pit-bull terriers, neither one blinking.

"Fine. If you don't want to dance, Sir Barnaby, I'll have to ask someone else. Your Grace? How about a spin around the great hall?"

At last the duke shifted his scowl to her. The sounds of other people entering the courtyard caused him to step back, although Barnaby remained in place. "This is not over."

"Nay. It is just beginning," Barnaby replied.

Laughter wafted from behind the hedges. A woman giggled. "Sir! Pray, return my hand at once!" Whoever she was, she did not sound as if she wanted her hand returned.

The duke turned and left.

Barnaby took a deep breath, then looked down at Sam. "Tell me," he said, smiling. "Would you really have danced with the duke?"

She relaxed, the danger past. "Yes. But he

was my second choice. You, sir, didn't seem to have much of an interest in me."

"Ah. There you are very wrong." His smile faltered, and then he began to lean forward, as if he would kiss her again. But the door opened, and a loud group of young men pushed into the courtyard, filling the garden with glimmering light and sound as they laughed amongst themselves. Barnaby straightened. "Besides, the duke is not a very good dancer. "

"Why does that not surprise me?"

With that he took her hand and led her back inside to the music.

King Edward watched the festivities with great delight, applauding the acrobats as they tumbled across the floor and landed at his feet.

"Excellent!" he shouted, nodding as one of his ministers offered to refill his wine goblet. He then gestured for the music to continue.

His sister Elizabeth sat to his right in her own chair, a place of honor but conspicuously less grand than the royal throne. She seemed slightly ill at ease, as if her position was but a momentary reward. Of course that was precisely the case.

Edward reached for another honeyed fig, his eyes scanning the room. Was it possible that only a few weeks ago, he had all but embraced the notion of death?

"Ha!" He made the exclamation aloud, and several of his courtiers turned and smiled hesitantly. Gone was the pious youth with the red-rimmed eyes and otherworldly air. Here was a vibrant prince full of robust vigor.

He smiled at a young woman toward the middle of the hall, and nodded over his fist full of figs. She blushed charmingly and returned his smile.

"By God, but life is good!" Edward announced to no one in particular.

Elizabeth looked up and smiled, then glanced away, her smile fading just slightly.

There was a fanfare, and a troupe of performers resplendent in all their gaudiness entered. A man sang with a voice as sweet as nectar, a ballad of love and longing. The next song was a jolly tune of love and conquest, much more to the king's liking and present temperament.

The king pounded his hands together when the three-legged bear was brought before him. The same bear had performed years earlier for his father. Now the bear, his muzzle gray, walked in limping circles. Everyone laughed at the sight, the ruffle about his neck stiff and purple. Everyone knew it was not within the bounds of the law for a nonroyal to wear purple, punishable by flogging. Yet they also knew their young king enjoyed a good joke, as did his father before him.

The trainer of the bear had taken a risk, and was rewarded with hearty laughter. Only the bear seemed wary.

"Your Highness," the deep voice whispered in his ear.

"Northumberland," Edward replied in more of a groan. "Leave us be. We wish to enjoy ourselves this evening."

"I have news that Your Majesty may find interesting."

Edward watched the bear push a ball with his nose, then do a handstand. The trainer danced about the animal, colorful ribbons swirling from his cap and sleeves.

"Later." The king waved his most powerful adviser away and took another sip from the silver goblet. His thumb rubbed against a large flat ruby set into the goblet, and he grinned. The smooth surface of the stone was most pleasing.

Life was very good indeed.

"Lady Sam and Sir Barnaby Fitzpatrick were together in the courtyard." The duke was unable to keep the edge of glee from his voice.

"What say you?" Edward turned and faced Northumberland for the first time that evening.

"I fear the two conspire to do His Majesty harm."

The king looked at the duke for a long moment, the bear forgotten. "Nonsense."

"Have a look, Your Highness." The duke tilted his head slightly to the right.

Sam and Barnaby stood by a huge, gold-draped column. He was, gesturing as he spoke, and she was nodding at his words. Then she put her hand over his, and Barnaby bent his head down.

From every other angle in the hall, it was clear that they were at least a foot apart. But there was a unmistakable sparkle in her eyes, an expression that no one had seen before on the face of young Lady Sam.

From where the king sat, the distance and slant of the dais from the couple, it looked very much like a kiss.

"Do you see, Your Highness?" The duke was unable to hide his smile. From the king's expression, first confusion, then disbelief, it was obvious that he did, indeed, see them.

Northumberland watched to see what would happen next. And as he had so hoped, the young boy king had a temper just like his late father, Henry VIII. Of course the duke had seen flashes of that temper before, when the king was a child. Now that the young monarch was in better health, that wrath could be used and honed.

He knew very well that as long as that fury was turned in another direction, it would not be aimed at him.

The duke smiled. This would be most enjoyable, to play the king against that guttersnipe Lady Sam and that Irish upstart Barnaby. Once again it was like the old times; he was in control.

Soon he would be in complete control, and this time it would not slip from his fingers.

The duke was again on familiar ground.

Sam touched Barnaby's hand. "That must have hurt," she said, tracing the jagged scar on his palm.

"Yea, it did." His voice was a husky whisper. "But no longer. I was but a boy. Scars heal."

The world beyond them seemed to be one bright blur as his fingers closed over hers.

How could this be happening? Such a glorious feeling to be with him, especially after the horrible words of Northumberland.

Had she really caused so much unhappiness?

She would try not to think about that right now, for she was there, with Barnaby.

She closed her eyes for a moment. This was more than a crush. This was something more powerful, more amazing.

"Sam." The way he said her name was like a velvet caress. She could stand there forever with him. Just stand and be happy.

"Lady Sam, Sir Barnaby." Someone was stepping between them. It took her a moment to realize it was Lady Jane.

Before they could speak, Jane continued. "Please, Sam. Follow me. I wish to retire."

"Oh, Jane," Sam replied dreamily. "Mind if I stay?"

"The king is displeased. I know not why, but I have an idea. Do not argue."

Barnaby withdrew his hand and pulled his gaze from Sam, looking toward the king and Northumberland. His former schoolmate's expression was blank, but his lips were set in a thin line and his eyes were mere slits. He knew that expression well. The king was furious. "Thank you, Lady Jane."

"What's going on?" Sam was confused and more than a little disappointed. Here she was, in the middle of a fabulous moment with a fabulous guy, and now she had to leave.

"Go with Lady Jane." Barnaby nodded. Even as he stepped away, his eyes retained the same faraway glaze she knew her own must have. "I will see you later."

"The king is angry," Jane repeated to Sam.

Barnaby bowed to both of them, then, suddenly, he turned his back and left, weaving through the crowds, pausing to speak with this courtier or that young knight.

"Did I do something wrong?" Sam asked. Other than destroying the nation, she added to herself.

"Nay. My cousin Elizabeth beckoned me to her side and told me she suspects Northumberland is intent on mischief."

"Oh," she replied distractedly, still watching Barnaby's broad back as he walked away.

"Elizabeth will tell the king you are unwell, and that I have taken you abed. Come."

As she was being pulled away, she caught one last glimpse of Barnaby. As if he sensed her location, he looked up and their eyes met briefly. A smile flickered there in his expression, then he turned back to his conversation. Whatever he said caused the cluster to laugh riotously, one gentleman slapped him on the back.

Within minutes, Sam was all alone, in her chamber. The distant music still played. For her, though, the evening was over.

Edward had never experienced such an emotion. It was not particularly pleasant.

When he had been ill, events occurring about him had seemed vague and well enough handled by others. First there had been Protector Somerset, then Northumberland. Now he felt a sickening sense of unease, as if he should do something decisive, but was not sure what that something should be.

For all of his learning, for all of the famous tutors who had been at his side since he could remember, he still was not certain of how to be a good king. He had been so young, there seemed time for him to learn. And in the meanwhile, Northumberland would do all the work, the difficult tasks that the king would eventually learn.

Then last fall he became ill. He had always enjoyed good health, other than the usual diseases of childhood. He even escaped death when the Sweat had spread through the court.

When he became ill, all that changed. The most vital element in his life had suddenly become preparing for his death. Life as a king, and a king facing increasing tension, even rebellion, was far more difficult than preparing for death.

Far more frightening as well.

Then there was the issue of Sam. Atop all else he needed to sort out his feelings about Lady Sam. How could one strange girl create such havoc within his kingdom? Within himself?

Then there was Barnaby, his closest friend, the person he loved and trusted most in the world. Barnaby alone had never let him down, had never betrayed any greed for power or wealth.

The mere thought of Barnaby and Sam alone together made his stomach tighten.

"We will continue this discussion in the morn," he declared as he watched the ceremonious ritual of his bedtime. Silk bedclothes were fluffed, pillows propped, the sheets made comfortable with a silver warmer.

Northumberland shook his head. "Nay, Your Majesty. It is imperative we discuss the matter now. For I fear that even as we speak, the parties in question are plotting against your royal person."

"There is no one we trust more than Sir Barnaby. He is our most favored companion."

"He is a foreigner," Northumberland stated flatly. "Do not forget that he comes from a foreign shore. He came here unwillingly."

"He was but a child!"

"Yea, he was. Think you not he has pondered his fate long and hard? The child torn from the breast of his family at such a tender age? Denied his identity?"

Edward paused for just a moment. This was unpleasant, very unpleasant. "He has forged his own identity here."

"But how he must resent it, Your Majesty. How he must wonder about his fate, at how he had no choice but to play the role of companion to the royal heir. Did he have brothers and sisters in Ireland?"

"We know not."

"Does his mother yet live?"

Edward did not answer.

"He has been away in France, Your Majesty. You know not what sorts of people he has associated himself with. With whom he has trusted the secrets of this nation."

"Barnaby is my closest friend. He has always

been my most trusted, most faithful. . . . Has he not? And he wrote to me faithfully during his time in France. I also heard reports . . ."

"From where did those reports come? How can the king know what a subject does in a distant land?"

Northumberland watched the king's eyebrows draw together. He was thinking. And better yet, he was worried.

"Your Highness, forgive me. But you have not had an easy time. It is most difficult for a prince in your most elevated position to make friends."

The privy servants continued to ready the king's chamber for bed, moving swiftly and surely and silently as an evening breeze.

Northumberland watched his king with practiced calculation. He knew precisely when to make his next move.

"And what of Lady Sam?"

Edward stopped and stared at the duke. Those thoughts had been swirling in his own mind, but he had tried to dismiss them. What would Northumberland say if he knew how she appeared in his chambers, as if from thin air? That she was an angel? At least, he had thought she was an angel.

Perhaps she was not. Perhaps she was,

indeed, all of those things Northumberland thought of her.

"What mean you?" Edward asked.

"What know you of her history?"

A servant offered the king a goblet, which he waved away without looking at it. "Tell me your thoughts, Northumberland."

"I wonder that the two have such an easy camaraderie, yet from all accounts had not met ere this evening. Fitzpatrick was abroad. Lady Sam arrived from we know not where." He paused for effect, watching the expression on the king's face, the confusion, the beginnings of doubt. He waited for his words to sink in before he continued. "In truth, Your Highness, I fear she is an agent from Ireland."

"Nonsense."

"What know you of her history? You know what she has told you, what she wished you to believe. Naught of the precise detail, of her people and her life. Are there not some portions of her tale that seem curious? That make little or no sense?"

Edward swallowed. He did not wish to tell Northumberland all, but perhaps just a bit of what had happened. "Yea. That is true. She appeared as if from nowhere and will not reveal to us her history."

Again Northumberland allowed the suspicions to take root, to settle into the king's mind as if they had been his own thoughts. Then he continued in a low voice. "Yet think, Your Majesty. If a foreign element was to attempt an uprising, how best to do it? Why, from within of course! With smiles and charm and pleasing manners. Is not Barnaby of noble birth in Ireland? And of Lady Sam, well—nothing is known."

Edward said nothing.

"Your crown is not certain, Your Highness. There are elements abroad and within who wish to make your sister Mary queen. Perhaps Lady Sam is of that faction."

"Why would she make me better, only to topple me? And why would Barnaby wish to do me harm?"

"This is a cruel world," Northumberland shook his head with theatrical tragedy.

"So what do you suggest?" The undecided Edward was back, the frightened boy looking for firm guidance. He felt his face grow hot with the shame of what was happening. He was king!

Still, he did not know what to do next. He needed help, a father figure. "So what do you suggest?" Edward repeated to the duke. The urgency in his voice was clear, music to the older man's ears.

"Well, Sire," Northumberland said as he stroked his beard. He acted as if he hadn't planned his words hours before. His tone was calm, confident. "I suggest you take them to the Tower of London. In that edifice they can be watched."

"The Tower?" Edward asked. "Where? In the royal apartments?"

Northumberland shrugged. "Perhaps. But there are lodgings more secure there. Ones with thick doors. Pleasant enough, and we will allow them a pretty space from which to enjoy the outside air. Not together, of course, but alone. And there I will question them most gently. And then, please God, we will have whatever nagging fears calmed."

"They will not be harmed?" Edward cleared his throat. "It is just that, well—as you know my father turned the Tower into a rather unsavory place. A fearful place. They will not be harmed, will they?"

"Of course not! And should I find any unpleasant news, you will be informed immediately. Their punishment, whatever it should be, will of course be ordered by your most benevolent person. But it will be fitting, in accordance to the law. Remember, Your Highness, you are the law."

"Well . . ." Edward was suddenly exhausted. "Perhaps that is a good notion. To question them—to gently inquire. That cannot harm them, can it?"

"Of course not! Why, it is the prudent course of action, Your Majesty! It is the princely course of action. I daresay your late father would be most pleased by his son's wise command."

"Do you think so?"

"Indeed!"

"Very well, Northumberland. You have my leave to question them tomorrow."

"I fear we must make our move now, Your Highness."

"Now? At this hour?"

"We need to catch them unawares, so they are unable to come up with a story together. It is vital that we move swiftly and certainly."

"Allow them to sleep," the king said softly. "Allow them one night of peace before their world is tipped upside down."

"Nay. Now. Or, I fear, it will be too late."

"Sir Barnaby is my closest friend. Never has he been untrue."

"Sire," Northumberland whispered close

to the king's ear, "history is littered with betrayal. The mightier the king, the greater the treachery."

"Yet . . ."

"Think of what your father would do. The great King Henry! And you are his son, his only son. Thus, unfortunately, comparisons are made. One would not wish them to be unfavorable, would one? Nay. Think again of your father. Did he not preserve a great kingdom for his son? Would you destroy that kingdom, undo in a matter of weeks this most hallowed empire? Will you be remembered as the boy king who allowed the mightiest land in the world to slip from his fingers like a child's plaything?"

A flash of anger sparked in Edward's eyes. His lips were pressed together, pursed into a thin furious line.

"Do it, then. Do it at once."

Northumberland felt a wave of relief flow through him, hot and powerful and utterly intoxicating. It was difficult to keep his voice calm and even, but, of course, he succeeded.

"It is a responsibility I shall hold most sacred. Now, Your Majesty, you seem weary. I will leave you. Good night."

Northumberland backed from the room, bowing.

Edward slipped into bed, and the heavy velvet curtains were closed to protect him from unwelcome drafts. The cloths, no matter how thick and sumptuous, though, could not protect him from his rioting thoughts.

He had known Barnaby most of his life and loved him like a brother. But Northumberland was uncomfortably correct. History was full of monarchs felled by their closest companions, their most trusted friends.

Lady Sam, of her he knew even less. She appeared in his room like an angel, but was she? Or had he been drugged into a stupor?

Lately she had been acting in a peculiar fashion. She wasn't as attentive, as if her mind were elsewhere.

Perhaps her mind had been on Sir Barnaby. On their plot. On his arrival from France.

Of course, Edward himself had ordered Barnaby back from France. Still, it was suspicious. Very suspicious indeed.

In the morning he would find out the truth. He rolled over and closed his eyes.

The king did not sleep well that night.

Chapter 9

Barnaby Fitzpatrick listened to the young man with disbelief.

"There must be some other reason they spoke so," he said, wiping his hand over his mouth, which had suddenly gone very dry. "Some mistake. Mayhap they were speaking of another." But even as he uttered the words, he knew there had been no mistake, no error. He walked over to the window and looked out into the darkness beyond, illuminated only by torches and lanterns swinging in the hands of the king's guards. "Never have I so much as held a disloyal thought toward my king. Never."

The servant nodded in agreement, stepping next to Fitzpatrick. "All who are familiar with you know that." He lowered his voice, fully aware of the danger he was posing to himself, even his family by telling Sir Barnaby of what he just overheard in the king's chamber. "Yet it was my duty to refill the royal goblet for His Majesty's pleasure. I was closer than anyone there, save the speakers themselves. And I would swear on all I hold sacred this is a true account of what transpired. 'Tis Northumberland's doing."

Barnaby stared into the young man's eyes and saw the honest concern there. Placing a hand on the servant's shoulder, he said simply, "I know not how to thank you."

"You have always been kind to me, Sir Barnaby. As has the Lady Sam. I can scarce believe what I heard, but I do fear for your life, and for that of the lady."

"Lady Sam." Barnaby breathed her name. "She does not deserve to be associated with me, with my downfall. She is guilty only of not knowing the treachery of the court, and that is all. My shame should not be visited upon her."

"But, sir, from what I overheard, Northumberland is every bit as eager to be rid of her as he is to be rid of you."

Barnaby said nothing, staring blankly out the window. No matter what the servant proclaimed, Barnaby was certain Sam's danger was his fault. Should anything happen to her, should she be harmed in any way . . .

He shook his head. He would not allow it. No matter the cost to himself, he would make sure she was safe. "And you are certain Northumberland will move tonight?"

The boy nodded.

"Then there is no time to waste. Know you where the Lady Sam slumbers?"

"Yea, my lord."

Barnaby paused for just a moment, wondering how all of this could have happened so quickly. Just that afternoon, only hours earlier, he had been praised for his diplomatic skill in France. The letters he had received from his king had been full of benevolent gratitude. He had been in favor, of that he was certain.

Now he was to be taken to the Tower.

He had seen it occur with others, of course. But in those cases, the shifting tides of favor had seemed to come on slowly. All had been aware of the pending turmoil, save for the victims themselves.

Now it was happening to him. How many others, besides the kind young servant, knew what was afoot? Of those people, how many would have risked all to warn him?

"Once more, thank you, friend. You will be well rewarded," he said to the servant. "And may I impose upon you for another favor?"

Without hesitation the servant nodded, and Barnaby outlined his plan.

Sam was deep into a strange dream.

She was flying, but not in an airplane or even in a hang glider, but with her arms acting as wings. Below her was the English countryside as she had seen it during the royal progress. There were flashes of beauty, of the rolling meadows or the magnificent gardens of some of the estates. Mostly, though, the view from above was horrific, of beggars and vagabonds, poor people being punished for their poverty in the market square pillories, of sick and homeless children in rags.

In her sleep she tossed from side to side. Some of the people in her dream were throwing things at her, rocks and stones. One frightening-looking man with a missing eye heaved a stick at her, tossing it like a javelin.

"Witch! Witch!" The people were calling to her, and someone had a torch.

"No," she murmured.

But they continued to throw anything they could, and the man with the torch stood below, smiling, waiting for her.

Then she began to fall, the earth rising fast, and suddenly below, waiting for her on the ground, sneering, was the Duke of Northumberland.

"No!"

And someone was there, holding her in his arms.

"Sam, you must awake."

She heard his voice as if from a long, hollow tunnel. "Sam, come."

Then she woke up. It was completely dark, and for a moment she thought she was still dreaming.

"There is not time to dress," he said.

"Barnaby?"

"Yes. Come."

"What's happening?"

"Northumberland has issued an arrest warrant for the two of us."

Suddenly she was fully awake. "Are you sure?"

"Absolutely certain. Do you have a cloak within this chamber?"

"No . . . wait. Please. How do you know there's a warrant for our arrest?" She felt like a character in a play, asking about the arrest warrant.

"One of the king's privy servants alerted me. I had once done him a small kindness. He came to my chamber to warn me of the danger. We must be gone now, before sunlight. There is a horse waiting just beyond the gate."

"I don't know how to ride a horse."

"Fine. I will ride. You will sit."

They bumped heads in the darkness, and Sam fumbled for a candle.

"No, Sam. No candle. We do not want the light to be seen."

"But my clothes, my shoes. Let me find the ring the king gave me. Lady Jane said that if ever I'm in trouble to send the ring to him and that might help."

"Not in this case. Northumberland is acting under orders of the king himself."

Sam ignored him and felt the bedside table in the darkness for the ring. She then slipped it onto her thumb.

With that Barnaby placed his own cloak over her shoulders. "Pray, be silent. At least until we reach London."

"We're going to London?"

"Shush. Yea," he whispered. "It is the nearest port. And from there we will take a boat to France. My ties there are fresh."

France, she thought crazily. Great. She'd always wanted to go there.

Holding his finger over her lips for silence, he slowly opened the door. The halls were empty. Then they moved as quietly and as quickly as they could, his arm around her over the cloak. All she wore was her nightgown from home and her silver necklace.

"Ouch," she hissed when she stubbed her toe. She hadn't had time to put on her shoes.

But still they ran, down a back staircase, outside along the hedges. Barnaby had timed it so they reached the gate when the guards were changing shifts. As the men exchanged words and brief orders, they slipped through in the darkness.

The horse was waiting, just as he had instructed the servant, and without speaking Barnaby threw her on the heavy leather saddle, then jumped up behind her. With just a click of his tongue and a light tap with his boot, they were off.

How come riding horses looked so easy in the movies? Why didn't they ever mention how bumpy it is, how smelly the horse can be? Or how darned uncomfortable saddles can be?

She tried to hold on to the horse's mane, but that didn't help. There was a ridge on the saddle, and finally she clutched it to steady herself.

After what seemed like hours, Barnaby relaxed in the saddle and eased his hold on her shoulders. She hadn't noticed how hard he'd been gripping her until then, but her shoulders ached, her teeth still felt as if they were rattling with every clump of the horse's hooves.

Dawn was just emerging over the hills, lighting their way.

"How fare you?" he asked at last.

"Tired and cold," she admitted. He readjusted the cloak over her shoulders.

There were so many things she wanted to say, but she was still perplexed by their sudden exit. How had this happened so quickly?

"Had we waited for daylight, we would soon be in the Tower," he answered as if he had read her mind. "I apologize for the unseemly haste, Lady Sam."

"Oh," she said so softly, he couldn't have heard. Then she spoke up, "Wouldn't it have been easier and safer for you to leave me behind?"

He said nothing, then, "Perhaps. But I could not leave you behind."

"Why not?" She turned to face him, really looking at him for the first time since the night before. His gaze was fixed straight ahead, his eyes searching the road before them for any signs of danger, any indication that something was wrong.

And then he gazed directly at her. "I do not know why I couldn't leave you behind. Perhaps because I have a strong sense that leaving without you would have a terrible ten-year consequence."

Before she could reply, he patted a leather bag hanging on the left of the saddle. "In here is a parchment that will assure you safe passage on the *Fleur de Lise*. It's the boat I took to and from France, the crew is yet intact. Should anything happen to me . . ."

"What do you mean?" That notion frightened her, that he would be harmed.

"Just should we be separated, you must find the ship. It will not be difficult, anyone can point it out to you. Do not wait for me, but present this parchment to the captain. You will sail immediately and be safe."

"But what about you?"

"I will find my way. Do not worry." He looked up, as if he had seen something. Then he smiled. "A hare. Look," he pointed, and she saw a little brown rabbit hopping behind a tree. Then it hopped out and hid behind another tree.

Sam was watching the rabbit when he continued, "Have you ever been to London?"

"No. No, I haven't." She swallowed, somehow

confused and pleased all at once.

He then told her all about London, of the shops and the many bridges. Of the great cathedrals and churches, grand homes and crowded streets. Barnaby laughed, a rich and wonderful sound as he spoke. She simply listened as he described all of the gates in London.

"There's Bishop's Gate, Moor Gate, Newgate. Many bridges as well. Holborn Bridge, just beyond Newgate. There's the Knight's Bridge. My favorite, for what reason I know not, is the Cow Bridge."

"The Cow Bridge?"

"Yea. It is somewhat less grand than the others, just a little wooden bridge that goes from Tyburne to . . ."

Then he stopped. She was about to ask more about the bridge when he very gently placed his hand over her mouth.

Until then she hadn't really felt a sense of danger. Everything had happened so quickly, there hadn't been time to be afraid. Also Barnaby had made this all seem like some sort of adventure. On purpose, she realized then.

Of course they were in danger. They were to be thrown in the Tower of London.

His hand tasted salty in her mouth, then, slowly he removed it.

"Come," he said softly. He dismounted the horse first, then reached up for her, helping her into his arms. The horse acted agitated, huffing and striking at the dirt road with a front hoof. Puffs of hot breath billowed from its nostrils.

"Good boy," he said, patting the animal's flanks.

Barnaby gazed at Sam for a brief instant. "Lady Sam, rest you behind that stone wall."

"What are you going to do?"

"I heard horses behind us. We're being followed. Here." He gave her the saddle bag. "Now go."

"Wait a minute. I didn't hear anything."

"Go!" His intensity stunned her, and without further questions she took the leather bag and went over to the small stone wall. She tossed the bag over, then climbed over herself, scraping her shin on the rocks.

Where would they hide the horse? There was no way it could be concealed behind the wall, which was less than four feet high and . . .

Then she realized what Barnaby was doing. He hefted the saddle over his shoulder, a huge, heavy ornate wooden and leather thing with straps. With a brief rub of the horse's mane, he slapped it on the rear.

"Go, boy," he said, but the horse did not move. Instead it just looked at Barnaby, its big brown eyes showing betrayal, confusion.

"Get on!" He slapped the horse hard, and it finally galloped away without looking back.

Barnaby watched for a moment as the horse ran across a field. Then he looked down the road behind and hopped over the wall himself.

"That was your horse?"

He settled the saddlebag by the saddle, then peered over the fence.

"That was my horse. I've had him since I was a lad, since I first came to these shores."

"I'm sorry," she said, not knowing what else to say. "I'm sure you'll get him back."

"I doubt that very much."

Suddenly Sir Barnaby Fitzpatrick, the big, handsome knight, seemed to be exactly what he was—a teenage boy whose pet had just run away.

"We should have ridden harder," he said to himself. He glanced over the wall, squinting against the sun, then turned back. "Faster. I thought they would wait until later in the morning to follow. That they would check the chambers at Hampton first. They should have assumed we were yet within the palace gates. Not here. This is a small road. The main one veers off. How could they have . . ."

All at once he stopped speaking, and his face drained of color.

Sam waited for him to explain, but he did not. Finally she asked "What's wrong?"

Barnaby turned toward her, his expression one of pure pain. "The servant"—he shook his head slowly—"he must have told Northumberland all. He must have been paid by the duke, to report our movements. Then I paid him myself. How handsomely he was rewarded. Oh, Sam, I am a fool."

"What are you talking about?"

He leaned against the stone wall and closed his eyes. "I pray God they pass, that my stupidity has not cost you your life." An unexpected wry chuckle escaped him as he opened his eyes. "He is brilliant, you know. He reckoned correctly, that the simplest escape route for us would be to trace my recent path to France. He knows the ship is still at port in London and that I am familiar with the crew. By now Northumberland has convinced the king that I was engaged in some sort of treasonous endeavor while there. And what I told the servant will but confirm to the king that we were in a plot together. That we have planned to escape to France. Forgive me. Please, forgive me."

The horses were moving closer, but he didn't seem to care. Sam touched his arm. "Maybe the horses you heard weren't people trying to follow us. Maybe just other folks traveling on the road to London . . ."

"Hush!" His hand was up, and he pushed her head lower behind the stone fence. Then she could hear it. The thundering of hooves.

All at once, she was terrified.

He, too, lowered his head. "Shush," he whispered. "All will be well. Think of this as a game." And then, improbably, he smiled.

She swallowed. Even through her rising panic she realized he was trying to ease her fears, that her apparent fear had caused him to rally, if only to keep her silent. She smiled back, but she could see by the shine in his eyes that he, too, was afraid.

Then the soldiers came. There was a small space in the wall between two rocks that allowed her a clear view of the road, and there seemed to be dozens of them. They rode by with leisurely speed, as if confident of catching their prey. Clouds of dirt swirled as they passed, obscuring her vision.

Suddenly a command was barked, and they stopped.

"No," she heard Barnaby whisper, hoping the soldiers would do as he commanded. "Go on," he urged.

A soldier dismounted. Then another.

Barnaby turned to her. There was a strange expression on his handsome face.

"Remember the parchment and the king's ring. London is straight ahead, not many miles. Wait for them to take me. Then go beyond the field, running low and swift. Do not stop. When you reach the ship, have them set sail at once. There may yet be time if I can distract them and keep them at bay."

She nodded, biting back the urge to ask when they would next meet, what would happen next.

"You will know when to run," he repeated. "I will cause a distraction. Stay low. Keep your gown close, don't let it billow out. Go over there, move from hedge to hedge."

"What are you doing?"

He didn't look at her when he answered. Instead he stared ahead, over the wall.

"It is my fault that you are in this position. Pray, allow me to do my best to correct my grave error."

"Don't be silly, Barnaby. We . . ."

Before she could continue, he stared directly into her eyes. His gaze, so very green and lucid, was piercing, so potent she gasped. "Do this for me. Promise me, Sam."

A breeze blew his hair, tousled it like a gentle, invisible hand. She searched for something to say, some grand statement, but all she could do was look back at his face, his handsome face, and nod. She was rewarded with a brief smile.

Then he moved ahead, crouching against the stone fence. How could he move so fast?

He turned back and grinned at her, as if this would be the biggest joke of all. Then he stood up and walked calmly over to the soldiers.

What was he doing?

Sam just sat there, staring. Stunned. They gathered around him, closing in. He could not escape, even if he tried. They took his sword and began to bind his hands.

She held the silver charm in her hand, watching.

Then one of the soldiers, the man in front with the biggest plume on his helmet, hit him. Hard.

"No," she whispered. "Oh, no. Please . . ."

Barnaby was hit again, but he remained

standing. She knew she was supposed to run. This was the distraction. But she couldn't.

The silver charm seemed to be heating up, growing ever warmer as she clutched it in her hands.

"How I want to go home," she cried, tears spilling down her cheeks.

One of the soldiers heard her, for he spun in her direction, his eyes narrowed as he surveyed the fence.

Barnaby shouted. Whatever it was he said made the soldiers furious, because the ones close enough to hear him all pointed their pikes and . . .

"No!" she heard herself shout. Rising to her feet, her hand still holding her charm, she saw them all turn toward her.

Barnaby. The expression on his face was raw, terrible, his features betraying feelings of pain and grief. He just stared at her hopelessly. He had risked everything for her escape, but it had all been wasted.

The reality hit her with sudden force. This was all real, all happening to them. She had the parchment in the saddle bag, proof that they were attempting to flee to France.

Now they would both suffer the consequences of their attempted escape, and it would be far worse than if they had remained at Hampton Court. The very act of fleeing would proclaim them guilty of whatever Northumberland chose to accuse them of. It didn't matter that they were innocent. From this point on they would be treated as convicted traitors. No such thing as innocent until proven guilty here, no such thing as a fair trial.

It was over.

Now they would be taken to the Tower, and as everyone knew, most people imprisoned in the Tower for political offenses never came out. Certainly not alive. Certainly not in one piece.

"I want to go home!" she sobbed in a voice filled with such anguish she barely recognized it as her own.

Then she felt dizzy. Shouts. They were shouting at someone. At her? Soldiers were coming toward her, she could see them in a blur. Barnaby was saying something. To her? To the soldiers? But she was unable to hear his words over the fierce howl of the wind.

A *whooshing* sound seemed to slam around her, like a loud tornado.

Then everything was silent.

She opened her eyes slowly. Her face was resting on something soft and warm.

Tired, so tired. But there were lights all around her.

Daylight. It must be daylight.

She sat up. For a moment she was confused, dazed. Then she realized where she was.

Back home. On her own bed. Before her was the open history book.

She was back home.

Chapter 10

Downstairs were the sounds and smells of dinner being made. Her mom was cooking something spicy and exotic, probably a new recipe from a magazine.

She looked around her room, trying to grasp what had happened. Her nightgown was dirty from the horseback ride with Barnaby, her bare feet were filthy. On her thumb was the clunky ruby ring that King Edward VI had given her. Finally she let go of the charm around her neck.

But something was strange about her room. It was different in subtle ways. The dresser was not hers. Instead of the beautiful chest of drawers she had been given a year earlier, this was a cheap-looking dresser with chipped white paint and babyish pink trim. Bright yellow pulls were on the drawers. A poster of someone she had never seen or heard was taped to her wall, a man in a two-toned shirt that looked like something from the nineteen fifties.

When had her mother ever let her tape stuff to the wall? She always had to be extra careful of the wallpaper and paint. Both were now a shade of pale green with some funny pattern. Sam slid from her bed to look closer.

"Poodles?" There were green poodles on her wall!

"Weird," she mumbled. Her father hated poodles. When had they decided to wallpaper her room with them?

Then she glanced over at her bookshelf. Instead of her Shakespeare and her novels there were rows of foreign paperbacks. Picking one up, she was absolutely perplexed.

What language was it? She studied French in school, but this seemed to be Spanish. There were a few books in English, but they were textbooks for people who speak Spanish. In the first chapter were simple sentences, such as "This is my nose," with a little girl pointing to her nose. Another one read, "This is a letter," and it was illustrated with an envelope and a letter, which she thought was rather confusing.

There were other English textbooks, more

advanced than the ones she had paged through.

Perhaps this was what her room had been like all along, but the time away had made her remember it differently. Maybe that was it.

"Samantha!" her mother called, giving the last vowel an odd roll.

"Coming, Mom." What she probably needed was a good dinner and an even better night's sleep. That's what she needed—and a hot shower. Of course.

She thought of Barnaby, but pushed the thought of him away. She couldn't deal with that now, not right now.

Stepping outside of her room, she stopped. The entire house was different! She was practically in the kitchen. The upstairs was gone—the house was all on one floor.

A television blared, and she followed the sounds to the living room. It wasn't a television, though, just a very old-fashioned–looking radio turned to a foreign-language channel. She guessed Jason thought it would be funny to drive everyone nuts by turning on a Spanish station.

Her mother was saying something. At least the voice sounded like her mother's. When Sam entered the kitchen, the woman there looked much older than her mom. She was wearing what appeared to be a calico housedress, like something Aunt Em would wear in *The Wizard of Oz.* And her slender, exercise-conscious mother was now more than matronly. She was at least thirty or forty pounds heavier than before. Also, she was older, so much older.

How long had Sam been away?

Her mother glanced up at her and said something. The problem was, Sam had no clue what her mother had said.

"Huh?" Sam asked.

Her mother repeated the same thing in the same language, brushing a wisp of her long gray hair out of her eyes as she spoke. She was clearly irritated.

"What's going on here, Mom? Why are you speaking like this? What happened to the house?"

Her mother stared at Sam, really stared at her, and said something else. An edge of nervous concern crept into her mom's tone. Sam could only shrug.

"Please, Mom. Speak English."

At that her mother said something that sounded like "Angleez?"

Then Jason came into the kitchen. "Jason, what's going on here?"

He was skinny and dirty, a hole in the shoulder of his striped shirt. His shorts were too small for him. In fact, *he* was too small for him—this Jason was at least four inches shorter than her real brother. He said something in the same language her mother was using.

Then Sam realized there were chickens in the backyard. The fridge was gone, replaced by an old-fashioned ice box. No dishwasher or microwave, only a funny gas stove. From the kitchen window she could see laundry hanging out to dry.

"What's happening?"

Jason and her mother looked at each other, then at Sam with complete confusion.

Panic gripped her, far worse than before, when she first landed at Edward's feet. "Um, I'm not hungry right now. Think I'll go back to my room." And with that she ran back into the strangely altered room and closed the door.

"Think, think," she said to herself, near tears now. Then she looked on her bed, at the history book still open there. Hesitating at first, she took a wary peek at the open page.

It was in English!

Next to it was a notebook and pen, full of writing in her handwriting.

The writing was in Spanish, though.

She paged through the notebook, and saw some sort of assignment for her English class.

"Oh." She sighed, understanding that the Sam who lived there took English as a second language.

"I can't think about that now," she said aloud. She needed to read the book on English history.

She pulled it toward her and read. There was the same painting of Edward she had seen before. He looked about the same as he had the first time she saw him, pale and weak, eyes red-rimmed. Then she turned the page, and there was a new painting, one she had never seen before. Edward as a robust adult. Edward on horseback. Edward going to war.

Swallowing hard, she read what had become of him, of everyone after she left. Edward ruled England for almost sixty years. But he was not a good king or a kind one. His subjects feared him. She skimmed down the page, looking for the major points.

Civil wars, uprisings. There were what Edward called "cleansings," rampages when he sent soldiers through villages to burn them down. He followed in his father's marital footsteps and had seven wives, beheading no less than four of them for reasons ranging from irritation with their singing voices to sudden infatuations with other women at court.

Edward had done this?

His sister Elizabeth married a knight, retired to the country, and died at the age of forty-three after having her seventh child. Princess Mary died a few years after Sam left court, having never married.

So there was never a Queen Elizabeth. Never a Golden Age in England.

There was no mention of Lady Jane, no mention of Barnaby Fitzpatrick. There was only a single brief paragraph on Northumberland.

Sam smiled at that. How furious Northumberland would be to realize he only rated a few sentences!

Reading on, she was stunned to find that Edward become such a terrible ruler. In spite of his father's giving him the best, the most enlightened education available at that time, he turned his back on virtually everything he had learned. Everything from the delicate art of diplomacy to how to please the common folk, from setting a good example to how to lead an army, Edward decided to follow only his own whims. He used England's wealth as his own personal bank, claiming private property as his own, writing new laws to give himself jewels or magnificent buildings or whatever else he so desired.

When Spain and France invaded England, there was no army to stop them, for Edward had dissolved the army, calling it expensive and unnecessary.

So Spain and France divided England among themselves.

King Edward was allowed to remain as a figurehead, but England became a mere colony of Spain and France. There was no Armada simply because the Spanish had no need—England was already theirs.

Other things did not exist. There was no William Shakespeare or Jonathan Swift. No brilliant Restoration dramas because there was no Restoration. Gradually all of England began speaking Spanish.

Sam could barely breathe as she continued reading.

The book's last chapter was a brief overview of the last few centuries. Although she found it difficult to follow, with references to people and events she was supposed to already know, the sketchy details were strange, even frightening.

There was no Industrial Revolution, no American Revolution. She looked at a map of the world, and North America was divided into dozens of small countries, similar to South America. From what she could tell on the map, the land that would have been Illinois and part of Indiana was a country called "Isabella."

She could see mentions of medical breakthroughs, but they were much later or different from what she remembered. Polio had remained a threat through the nineteen seventies. Airplanes were invented in France during the early nineteen twenties. Lightbulbs, from what she could tell in the book, were square and very expensive. She looked up and realized that in her own room, the overhead lighting was by oil lamp!

There was no mention of a Thomas Alva Edison, but there were other names of people she didn't know, Eduardo Hepta, a great leader of the country of Madrid, which seemed to be most of what Sam knew as California. There was some woman named Henrietta Spellez who sang and danced in the early 1960s.

It seemed from the history book that the North American countries did little more than squabble with one another and suffer in grinding poverty.

Finally Sam closed the book.

Had her brief visit back to 1553 changed everything?

Closing her eyes, she thought for a moment.

Northumberland had called the world of 1553 "a delicate balance." Every action impacted on the fragile balance and could cause it to become unstable, to topple. Sam had upset that carefully constructed balance.

That was the difference.

When she had first met the king, he was close to death. She saved him, and by saving Edward she changed the course of history.

Talk about a ten-year significance.

Could that have been it? As she thought she fingered the charm. It seemed to be warmer than usual, almost as if it had been heated on a stove.

The charm.

She froze. Of course, the charm! It must contain the magic that sent her back and forth! It had worked the first time when she so desperately wanted to be anyplace but home, when she was about to get yelled at for wrecking the BMW. The second time it was when she desperately wanted to go home, away from the turmoil of the soldiers.

That was it. Now it made sense.

Then maybe, just maybe, she could return for a short time, to right the wrong she had caused.

Maybe she could even save Barnaby!

Then she heard footsteps outside her door. Now, she prayed to herself, rubbing the charm as if it were a genie's bottle. Please. This has to work!

The charm grew warm, then hot. The familiar dizziness returned. She envisioned the hall at Nonesuch Palace where she had first seen Edward, of the sights and scents and feel of the place. Every detail she could recall throbbed in her mind. She felt herself tilting, the *whooshing* swooped over her.

Then she was in a large room. A fire crackled. A dog lay nearby. At the end of the room was Edward, just as she had first seen him. Sickly and pale, wrapped in a fur collar.

"I have been awaiting your visit," he said softly.

"I know," Sam said, barely able to contain her excitement.

It worked!

"You are an angel sent from God."

Sam nodded, and rose unsteadily to her feet.

"Have you seen my father and my mother?"

"I have indeed. I was just with them." Sam tried to make her voice sound as important as possible. "And they look forward to joining you. Oh, and your mother says it's okay about her brothers. It wasn't your fault."

"Your speech is most strange," Edward said just before a coughing fit overtook him. Then he smiled. "My mother is not angry?" Again, he coughed.

She waited for it to subside, not offering any comfort, which made her feel terrible.

She had to do this, though.

"No. She loves you and is proud of you, as is your father." Sam nodded with what she hoped could be passed off as an air of wisdom. Clutching at her necklace, she began to feel that dizzy sensation, and she knew she didn't have long now.

Then an idea came to her.

Quickly she held on to the charm and slipped off the silver necklace. "But before I go, there is a vital mission I must complete. Then I will again travel to the stars."

Why was she suddenly sounding like the captain of the starship Enterprise?

Without thinking further, she stepped over to Edward and handed him the silver necklace. The charm remained in her hand. "Do you have a companion named Barnaby Fitzpatrick?"

"Yes, I do!"

"Give this chain of silver to him. It is a gift to remind him of his home, of where he belongs."

Edward took it with solemn dignity, almost as if performing a religious rite.

Then something on her hand caught his eye. "Is that not my ruby ring?"

She forgot about the ring on her thumb. Would the ring make a difference, alter the situation in any way?

"Yes, it is your ring," Sam proclaimed.

"It is most valuable." Edward crossed his arms, the silver chain still in his hand. "Why are you wearing it?"

"I am wearing it because . . ." she began, pausing for effect while she racked her mind to come up with something decent. "I am wearing it to prove that I am your angel. How else could I have it in my possession?"

Quickly she yanked it off her thumb and handed it to him before he could realize that, in fact, her explanation made absolutely no sense.

She rubbed the charm. "I want to go home NOW!"

The king began to cough, and Sam felt herself slipping away. "Good-bye, Edward!"

He smiled weakly, the silver chain glittering in the dim firelight, the ruby ring in his hand. "Farewell, sweet angel!"

The room grew blurry, and she watched his face as she felt herself go dizzy, then she closed her eyes. The *whooshing* sound flew by her ears.

Then it was over.

Sam was almost afraid to look around her room. With only one eye open slightly, she took a small peek at the dresser.

It was her old dresser!

Opening both eyes, she knew immediately that she was back where she belonged, that everything was right again. Shakespeare was in his place on her shelf. The electric lights blazed with their customary taken-for-granted brightness and familiar round bulbs. Downstairs she could hear Jason's video game killing the alien forces on the oversize TV screen.

There was her history book, too.

It was open to the same page, of young,

sickly Edward. A notebook filled with her own handwriting—in English this time—was beside the book. There were his dates. Born, 1537. Died, 1553.

"Poor Edward," she said, reading that he was a brilliant, compassionate boy who might have become the greatest of kings.

"Or maybe not," she said, flipping the page.

Reading on, she learned that after Edward's death, Northumberland tried to secure the throne for his son Guildford and Guildford's new wife, Lady Jane Grey.

"Jane!" Sam shouted with excitement. Then a new sadness washed over her. Jane was beheaded, along with her husband and Northumberland.

Sam knew this was meant to happen all along. It was just so horrible to think of anyone hurting a girl as kind as Jane.

Queen Mary ruled for a few years, not very well or very wisely. Finally Sam could smile at the portraits of the greatest Tudor of them all, Queen Elizabeth. Her coronation painting was glorious, with her long hair flowing just as Sam remembered it. Only no daisy there, just stacks of glittering jewels and a crown. One of the jewels was the square ruby ring she had returned to Edward.

To think, the great Queen Elizabeth taught Sam how to dance the volta.

It was all there, the Armada, the triumphs. The literature and plays and music. Everything was restored.

Of course there was no mention of a certain knight, a certain Barnaby Fitzpatrick.

Had there ever been?

Just then she heard the front door open downstairs, and Jason's eager voice.

In English this time, wonderful, beautiful English.

Then she heard her dad.

"She did WHAT to my car?"

It seemed impossible, but all Sam could do was smile. She was home again, and maybe with a little luck she would be grounded for a very long time.

Her dad had been furious, but mainly relieved that she was all right, and that nobody had been hurt. Not only was she grounded, but she could not take her driver's test for another six months. In the meantime, her father took her out every weekend for humiliating driving lessons in the station wagon.

"Perhaps when you're thirty-five, you can

have another chance behind the wheel of the BMW," he had said.

He wasn't kidding.

Of course she probably would have been grounded until summer, but when she aced her history test the next morning, her parents were so delighted they un-grounded her.

The only one who wasn't surprised by Sam's perfect history final was Sam herself. Even Mr. Novack, her history teacher, was pleasantly surprised. He was especially impressed with the essay portion of the exam. Sam wrote a detailed account of the duke of Northumberland's ruthless quest for power. It was one of those essays that seemed to flow from her pen, as if someone else were dictating the words to her. She barely finished the exam by the time the bell rang. Mr. Novack even read the essay to the class, which was both embarrassing and exciting at the same time.

"I'm delighted to see you taking such a keen interest in English history, Sam."

"Thank you, Mr. Novack," she said at the end of the week, gathering up her books after class. "May I ask you a question?"

"Most certainly." He smiled, looking up from a stack of papers. Funny how much a teacher will smile once he detects even a glimmer of interest on your part in his subject.

"Do you know what happened to Sir Barnaby Fitzpatrick? He was Edward's whipping boy, later knighted. I can't find anything about him."

"Fitzpatrick, eh? That is a nice bit of trivia. Let me check with this book on the middle Tudors. Much more complete than the text you have. Let's see."

With that he pulled a massive volume from the shelf behind his desk. Flipping through the index in the back, he stopped. "Ah, here we go. Page four hundred thirty-eight."

He opened to the page and skimmed down, pausing. "Here we go. Sir Barnaby Fitzpatrick. Was sent to court as a hostage from Ireland. Interesting. Boyhood companion of the king. Was beginning to demonstrate a genuine talent for diplomacy. But it seems he was never heard from again after Edward died. He probably got mixed up in the Lady Jane Grey mess. Sorry I couldn't find anything else."

"That's okay. Don't know what I expected to find," she said softly. "Have a good weekend, Mr. Novack. And thank you." Sam just smiled as she left the classroom.

Everything was back to normal. Tonight was her belated sixteenth birthday party. She had postponed the one in April, simply because she wasn't in a party mood. Now that it was almost June, she still wasn't sure how she felt, but the birthday party was combined with an end-of-school-year bash.

It was a costume party, a "Come as You Were" theme, something a little different, a little unique.

She tried to get excited about her costume. Her mom had helped her make a rough variation of one of Lady Jane's gowns. Sam drew sketches of what she wanted and her mother nodded, attempting to create it on the old Singer sewing machine. Lori was going to be Lady Godiva in a flesh colored leotard and a long wig. Kevin the Hunk was coming as the Lone Ranger. Sam decided not to point out that the Lone Ranger was a character from fiction, not history.

Everyone was really psyched about her party.

Still, she couldn't help but wonder about a long-ago friend who had tried very hard to help her, a guy with the greenest eyes she had ever seen. She couldn't help but think of Sir Barnaby Fitzpatrick.

Lori grinned as she reattached the clump of balloons to the tree. The entire backyard was bedecked with crepe paper, balloons, and sparkly tissue. Lori had spent all afternoon on the decorations.

"Really, Sam! This will be the best party ever! Do you think we have enough dip?"

"Sure. Mom has more inside just in case." A few people had trickled in. The CD player was already cranking out songs loud enough to disturb the entire neighborhood. And Jason had been sent over to a friend's house to spend the night.

Even her hair was looking better. Not that it was visible under the cardboard headdress Sam had fashioned. It was much lighter than the real ones, and bobby pins were a vast improvement over the clips they had really used.

Her gown looked great, the blue polyester velvet more comfortable than the thick, uneven velvet of old. No corsets, no farthingales.

She had wrapped gold tissue around the trees in the backyard, recalling the gold cloth-wrapped columns at Hampton Court.

Sometimes she would pause and wonder why she occasionally longed for a place and time that had caused her so much fear, so much pain.

Still, though, somehow she couldn't erase the sadness that would creep up on her without warning. As difficult as it was to realize she would never have the chance to thank Barnaby, or to say good-bye, it was far more difficult not knowing what had happened to him.

Maybe he went back to Ireland and married some pretty girl. Nah, that wasn't a line of thought she wanted to pursue. Maybe he went back to Ireland and became a powerful chief just like his father.

That was better. Much better.

Or perhaps he went back to France. Or changed his name.

"Hey, Sam!" It was Brad and Jen from her homeroom. "Happy belated birthday!" They were dressed as Sonny and Cher, he in a furlike vest made by cutting up an old bathroom rug. She was wearing a waist-length black wig and long press-on fingernails.

Sam laughed as they all praised her gown.

It felt so great to be back home!

She looked over at the flower bed by the house. Hidden beneath the roses was the silver charm her mother had given her. Whatever it was about that thing, Sam knew it was too dangerous to keep.

Who knew what would happen next time?

She told her mother she lost it, feeling slightly guilty at the white lie—but it was the only thing to do, really.

The sun was beginning to set. Sam looked toward the horizon and up at the stars. The stars weren't nearly so bright as they had been at Hampton Court. The darkness not nearly so complete.

"Sam, he's here," Lori whispered. For a second Sam forgot where she was, excited that the "he" was Barnaby. Then Lori added, "Kevin the Hunk!"

Sam straightened and put on her best smile. The yard was packed now with her friends, kids from her classes, and some people she didn't know well but had seen around school.

"Ah, the belated birthday girl," Kevin said, leaning over to kiss her cheek. "Did you get your driver's license yet?"

Had his hair always looked so blow-dried? And had he always smelled of too much aftershave?

"Hi, Kevin. Nope. I have to wait a while." She tried not to sound disappointed and looked away. The combination of no license and a rather uninspiring Kevin the Hunk was downright depressing.

"Too bad." He smiled, and there was onion dip wedged between his teeth. "Maybe next weekend we can . . ."

She wasn't listening, instead she was looking around her backyard. Everyone was laughing, smiling, comparing costumes. Someone was dressed as a clown with a multicolor fright wig and a red ball nose. Another boy, this guy named Mike that Lori had a semicrush on, was wearing a cowboy outfit, twirling a plastic six-shooter and walking with bowed legs, as if he'd been on a horse for a month. Sally Adams was Whistler's Mother. Ben from her math class didn't know it was a costume party, so he borrowed a plaid blanket from Sam's mother and went as a Highland warrior.

Sam swallowed as she stood alone at the edge of the party. Funny, she thought to herself. Here she was back home, in her own yard, and still she felt out of place, a stranger. Of all the people there, she alone had actually lived the life of a person in the costume she was wearing.

People were beginning to dance. Her dad brought out another bowl of dip and chips and checked the tub filled with ice and soda to see if it needed restocking.

Kevin the Hunk waved at her from across

the yard, and limply, without much enthusiasm, she waved back.

Then there was a rustling in the hedges behind her. Great, she thought. Probably some couple making out.

With her parents peering out of the window all the time, she thought it best to see what was going on. All she needed was to get into trouble now, with summer coming and the BMW disaster still fresh.

"Okay, who's in there?" She reached in the bush, pushing aside a branch. Someone in dark clothing moved, uttering an oath she couldn't hear over the music.

"Come on. This isn't funny. Whoever you are, you're wrecking the shrub."

Leaning farther into the bush, she began to lose her balance—and suddenly she tumbled against someone.

"Oh, sorry!" She pushed against a familiar feel—thick velvet. And the scent, of horses. Of the outdoors and hay. And leather.

"Lady Sam?"

For an instant she thought she was dreaming. "Barnaby?" Sam whispered.

His voice grew stronger. "Sam? Pray God, may this be you!"

With a mighty tug, Sam pulled his arm, and

they both tumbled out from the bush. A dagger was clenched in one fist, and in the other was a broken silver chain.

Sam simply stared for a moment as Sir Barnaby Fitzpatrick blinked and glanced at the party, his expression one of dazed exhaustion. Still sprawled on the ground, his sword slung against his thigh, he said nothing. Then he turned to her and grinned. "Sam."

"Oh my God!" Her eyes stung with tears. "What happened? How did you . . ."

He shook his head. "I know not. One moment ago I was being taken to the Tower by Northumberland's men. I had just been told that my date of execution had been fixed for tomorrow morning at nine of the clock."

"Were you in the country? Escaping to London?"

"Nay," he replied slowly. "Yet I had a dream of that very nature." He sat up, returning the dagger to the sheath at his waist. "How be it that I know you, and yet we have never met?"

Sam was about to speak when Kevin the Hunk came over. "You okay, Sam?" He eyed Barnaby with suspicion, taking in his broad build and weapons.

"Yes, Kevin. Thanks. I'm fine."

Kevin hesitated, then walked back to the

onion dip, looking over his shoulder twice.

"I dreamed of you," Barnaby said as if Kevin had not just been there. "And then the king gave me this silver necklace, bade me keep it, that it was from an angel. And somehow I knew it was from you, Lady Sam, of whom I have dreamed so clearly."

Sam couldn't help but stare at him. He was even more handsome than she remembered, more alive and vibrant.

So he remembered her as a dream. For she never met him on her second trip, when she allowed Edward to remain ill. Still Barnaby held on to an element of what had occurred before, what might have been.

"Did you dream of me as well?" Barnaby asked.

That was easy to answer. "Yes," she said and smiled. "A lot."

"How came I here?"

"The chain. You must have been wishing to be with me and the silver worked for you as it worked for me."

"Aye," he said softly. "I confess I was frightened when the men came for me, for I knew these would be my last hours on earth. The sun had set already, and but one more sunrise would I see. One. I grabbed the chain, I know not why. But an image came to me then, of you. Of you being in some sort of danger, and of me thinking that 'tis too late to save myself. Save her. Save Sam. Make a distraction. Let her go home, to her home, to her family, safe and whole."

"And so you came here, to me," Sam whispered. "Safe and whole."

They simply looked at each other for what seemed like a long time. His green eyes flashed in the light of the backyard lamps. Behind her she was aware of music, of kids dancing.

"Hey, Sam." Lori tapped her on the back, and she jumped.

"Oh, Lori. Um, this is my friend Barnaby."

Lori smiled what Sam recognized as her flirtation grin. "Hi, Barnaby." She did a little shoulder roll she had been practicing in the mirror for the last few days. "Great party, isn't it?"

With that Barnaby rose to his feet, sword clattering, and assisted Sam to her feet. Then he bowed grandly over Lori's hand. "Good evening," he began. Then he did an almost comical double take as he saw that Lori, in her flesh-colored leotard and long hair wig, seemed to be completely naked.

"Nice costume, Barn," Lori said. "Did you and Sam plan this together?"

Barnaby was still unable to speak. "I . . ."

"Sort of," Sam said quickly. "Lori, could you see if there's enough salsa? We were running out a minute ago."

"Sure." Then she leaned to Sam. "He's gorgeous! Who is he? He must go to another school."

"Thanks, Lori," Sam gave her friend a gentle push, and a smiling Lori went to check on the salsa.

"Where am I?" he asked her.

"This may be hard to explain," she began. "You are in my place and time, and you are safe from Northumberland, safe from the king, safe from everyone."

He still seemed stunned, his gaze resting on people dressed as clowns or cowboys or ballet dancers. Before she could explain that it was a costume party, her mom came over.

"Hi, Sam," she said, staring at Barnaby.

"Mom, this is a good friend of mine, Barnaby Fitzpatrick. Barnaby, this is my mother."

Barnaby took her mother's hand and bowed. "Gentle lady, how good it is to—"

Sam interrupted. "Mom, Barnaby helped me with history. Believe me, if it hadn't been for Barnaby, I never would have gotten an 'A' on my final."

"Really?" Her mother seemed pleased. "You must be quite a tutor, Barnaby."

"Nay. I am not a Tudor. I am a Fitzpatrick."

"Oh, I see." But clearly her mother did not. "What a lovely accent you have, Barnaby. Where are you from?"

He looked at Sam, and she nodded for him to answer. "I was born in Ireland, but raised in England."

"Oh, how fascinating! Is your father some sort of businessman?"

"He is a chieftain."

Her mother appeared confused. "Pardon me?"

"A chief financial officer," Sam added. "Some company."

"I see," her mom said dubiously. "Well, welcome to the party. Help yourself to soda and chips."

Barnaby gave her his best court bow. "I do hasten to thank you, great lady, and—"

Her mother paused, then smiled. "You are most welcome." With one more glance at Barnaby, her smile became more genuine. "Fabulous costume! I'm going back inside. This music's giving me a headache."

Sam sighed.

Suddenly Kevin the Hunk was standing

beside them. "Hi, Sam," he said, staring at Barnaby.

"Hi, Kevin. This is Barnaby."

Kevin nodded a guy-like "hello," and Barnaby did the same.

"Hey, Sam. Did you get your license yet?"

"Nope. I just told you, I have to wait."

"Oh yeah." Kevin shifted. "I just heard Sam tell her mother that you helped her with history. Is that true?"

Barnaby gave him a wary nod.

"Listen, I'm about to be booted from the football team because I'm failing English history," Kevin whispered, embarrassed. "My dad will kill me—I'm supposed to be captain next fall."

"Kevin," Sam started to push him away. "Go have some more soda or something."

"Can you help me?" Kevin pleaded.

Barnaby frowned. "What mean you?"

Kevin grinned. "Hey, I love the way you talk, man! It's really cool! Bet the chicks really like it, eh? Anyway, if you could come over to my place for the weekend and help me with the history of Henry and all that, I'd be your pal forever."

"That's not a bad idea." Sam paused. "You could stay with Kevin and help him out, and he could teach you about being a guy here!" She turned to Kevin. "You see, Barnaby's sort of a foreign exchange student."

"My mom would love that!" Kevin exclaimed. "She loves all that PBS stuff!"

"Oh, and Kevin—most of Barnaby's clothes were lost. Could you lend him some? You're about the same size."

"Airline lose your luggage?" Kevin asked.

Barnaby glanced at Sam, and she smiled. "Yea, verily they did," he replied.

"Bummer, man. I lost my skis last year coming back from Aspen. Know what it's like. So I'll catch up with you later, okay? We'll catch a ride home with that dude over there dressed in a blanket."

"Most excellent, sir." Barnaby bowed.

"Can you teach me to talk like that, too? It's got to be a real chick magnet."

"Later, Kevin." Sam laughed, giving him a gentle shove. He gave a thumbs-up sign and went over to the chips.

Sam looked up at Barnaby.

"What just transpired?" he asked.

"I think you may have a new home," she said.

What would he look like in jeans and a T-shirt?

He was about to speak when the music changed. Sam had forgotten—she had borrowed some CDs from Mr. Novack, music he'd purchased at a Renaissance Fair in upstate New York.

Barnaby smiled, looking around the yard. "Where are the musicians?"

"Um, well. They're hiding right now."

"Lady Sam," he turned to her. "We never did dance."

"No, we didn't."

"Is that not a volta?"

"I believe it is," she said softly.

He took her hand. Everyone had left the middle of the yard, uncertain how to move to the strange, old-fashioned music.

Barnaby and Sam knew.

He led her to the now-clear space, her hand resting on the crook of his arm. They stopped and he faced her, bowing. She nodded graciously.

Then, suddenly remembering what was in his hand, he gave her the broken silver chain. "Here, I believe this is yours, Lady Sam."

She slipped it into her pocket. There was a slight pause in the music, then it began to pick up. And without any hesitation, they began to perform the intricate steps of the volta.

Silence descended over the party as everyone watched in amazement. The couple moved as if they had danced together for years, with ease and smooth certainty and obvious delight. When he lifted her, she felt she could soar to the sky, her arms as wings.

Then he twirled her, and she threw her head back with the sheer joy of the movement. He, too, laughed, his eyes focused only on Sam.

"He's incredible," she heard Tina Williams sigh.

"Who is he?" another girl asked.

"Hey, did anyone know Sam could do that?" Kevin the Hunk said to no one in particular, adjusting his Lone Ranger mask. "Do you think those are real swords on his costume? He's staying at my place, you know. He'll teach me that."

Sam heard nothing but Barnaby's humming to the music.

Queen Elizabeth had taught her well.

At the end of the dance, when the music stopped and his arms were still around her waist, she realized that all of her friends were clapping. A few whistled, and several "wows" were uttered in the night air. Her mother and father stood on the back steps of the porch, both with their mouths open in wonder.

As Barnaby Fitzpatrick grinned as men did in centuries past, Sam realized one thing.

She belonged.

With her high school friends, in this place where she had grown up. With her family. And with Barnaby, whom she knew without a doubt would prove to be a friend for the rest of her life. He had already proved so much more.

This was where she belonged.

All she could say, to Barnaby, to everyone, after the pure exuberance of the moment passed, was, "A volta rocks."

And it did.

Author's Note

Edward VI was only fifteen when he died in the summer of 1553. Over the centuries he has been portrayed as a pious child, stricken with tuberculosis and wasting away for most of his short life.

More recently, medical experts who have viewed the often sketchy records of the day have seen a robust boy who enjoyed unusually good health until several months before his death. Accounts of his last weeks indicate that he probably died of a sudden and intense respiratory infection. In other words, he had a bad cold that got worse.

Medicine in those days was far more likely to do the patient harm than good. Bleeding, applying leeches, purging (or making the patient vomit), and even doses of poison were considered state-of-the-art medical care. So had poor Edward been just a commoner, without a full team of court physicians, he would have stood a far better chance of surviving.

The thought of Edward's surviving is one of the wonderful "what-ifs" of history. Even Mark Twain couldn't resist wondering what if in his 1882 book *The Prince and the Pauper.* So I began to wonder, what if poor Edward also suffered from adolescent allergies? We all know kids with tons of allergies. Even now those allergies are difficult to diagnose and treat. What would happen to someone in the mid-sixteenth century, surrounded by dogs and furs and being fed all the things that would make him worse? That would certainly explain why he couldn't shake the terrible cold that took hold that spring. Without antibiotics, and with the barbaric medical care forced upon him, his fate would have been sealed.

But what if someone who knew the basics of treating allergies had arrived at court sometime during that spring? Not a doctor, but perhaps someone very much like you. Someone who knows that when you remove a dog, the person with allergies is likely to stop sneezing and coughing. If only Edward had had a brief chance to recover, he could have rallied and lived. He was young and had been strong. It's not an impossible what-if.

And what would that recovery do to a young, wealthy kid with the world at his feet? Think of the kids in those boy bands who suddenly become rich and famous. Then multiply that, for Edward was not only rich and famous, he was king of the most powerful kingdom in the world.

That would have to do something to a kid's head, don't you think?

The real Edward Tudor was a normal, healthy teenager until that final illness. He loved to participate in sports and tournaments, enjoyed music and dancing, and had a genuine fondness for flashy clothes. He was a precocious student, like his sisters and cousin Jane, and kept a chronicle, which seemed to be part diary, part school exercise. But had he lived, England would have been robbed of Queen Elizabeth. Sadly, it took a young boy's death to pave the way for one of the greatest eras of British history.

Edward had a whipping boy, an Irish lad named Barnaby Fitzpatrick, who was schooled by his side and was considered to be the young king's closest friend. But after Edward's death, the newly knighted Fitzpatrick seems to have vanished. If ever you happen upon an old, obscure book on British history, blow off the dust from the cover and check the index in the back. I know I will, always hoping to find something, anything, about the real fate of our mysterious Barnaby Fitzpatrick.

Perhaps the saddest story of all is that of Lady Jane Grey. The duke of Northumberland, along with Jane's parents, forced her to marry his youngest son Guildford in the spring of 1553. When Edward died, Northumberland proclaimed Jane the new queen against her will. Always conscious of her short stature, she wore her cork-soled shoes when the proclamation was read to add a few inches to her height. Her reign lasted only nine days before Princess Mary raised forces and seized power. Jane, whose only wish was to be left in peace with her books, was beheaded in the Tower, as was Northumberland, Jane's father, and Guildford.

You might want to check out the following books at your library, to start to imagine your own "what-ifs."

Edward VI by Jennifer Loach. Yale University Press, 1999.

Henry VIII and his Court by Neville Williams. Macmillan Company, 1971.

The Tudor Age by Jasper Ridley. Overlook Press, 1990.

Judith O'Brien

JUDITH O'BRIEN wrote and illustrated her first book in third grade, the gripping page-turner (all ten of them) *Little Lulu Goes to the Store.* Although the work won lavish praise from her parents, her big brother pelted her with snowballs. Years later, and a safe distance from her brother's snowballs, she wrote a second book, *Rhapsody in Time* (Pocket Books, 1994). Between the two works, she wrote for newspapers and magazines, including *Seventeen* and *YM*, got married, and had a son. Many books later, she now lives in Brooklyn, New York, with her son Seth and an ill-behaved mutt named Pepper.

IT WAS A BRILLIANT SCIENTIFIC BREAKTHROUGH.
A GENE THAT MUTATES THE MIND,
THAT GIVES A HUMAN BRAIN ACCESS
TO ALL COMPUTER SYSTEMS.

IT IS A DEADLY CURSE. IT CREATES PEOPLE
OF INCALCULABLE POWER, WHO MUST BE
DESTROYED BEFORE THEY CAN GROW UP.

IT IS A THRILLER THAT BLASTS YOU
INTO A MIND-BLOWING FUTURE....

HEX

SHE IS ALL-POWERFUL.
SHE MUST BE DESTROYED!

HEX: SHADOWS

SHE SHOULD BE DEAD.
BUT COMPUTERS ARE HARD TO KILL...
(COMING IN FEBRUARY 2002)

HEX: GHOSTS

THE GOVERNMENT WANTED THEM DEAD.
THE WORLD WAS NOT READY FOR THEM.
BUT NOW THEY ARE GOING
TO MAKE PEOPLE LISTEN.
(COMING IN JUNE 2002)

Published by Simon & Schuster

3115